## The Mafia had always ruled San Valdesto

They owned all the real estate and controlled all the politicians. The townspeople didn't like it, but they'd learned to live with it.

Then a giant power company made plans to build a nuclear generator very close to their homes—on Mafia-owned land that had been scheduled for lucrative redevelopment.

For the first time, the Mafia and the worried townspeople found themselves united in a common cause.

It was a very uneasy partnership!

**William Campbell Gault**

is also the author of
Raven House Mystery #18
**The Bad Samaritan**

*"It's a pleasure to read a
real mystery again. I couldn't
put it down."*
—Dorothy B. Hughes

Nothing much ever happened in San
Valdesto. The townsfolk were
peaceful and law-abiding—even if
some of them were retired Mafia
dons.

No one wanted to know about a
protection racket that terrorized the
area's shopkeepers. No one tried to
disband the local string of teenage
call girls. No one worried about the
drug dealers who kept the town's
schoolchildren happy. No one cared.

No one except Maude Marner—she
cared a lot. But she got killed for her
caring.

# THE CANA DIVERSION

## William Campbell Gault

A RAVEN HOUSE MYSTERY FROM
# W🌐RLDWIDE
TORONTO • LONDON • NEW YORK

For Ellie Lazarus

———————————◆———————————

Raven House edition published April 1982

Second printing April 1982

ISBN 0-373-63029-8

Printed in Canada

1

INCIDENTS, COINCIDENCE.... If Jan hadn't gone to jail, Joe Puma might never have known I was in town. And if he hadn't learned that, he couldn't have told his wife, and I never would have become involved in his shoddy business.

The above is confusing; let me put it into sequence.

I had this sidehill birdie putt of about nine feet on the thirteenth green. After two consecutive presses, I figured it was a sixteen-dollar putt. I was playing with two doctors and a lawyer; sixteen dollars meant nothing to them. But I had become solvent only recently. With my economic conditioning, sixteen-dollar putts will always be scary.

I gave it a lot of thought and surveillance, as the pros on the boob tube do, and was walking back to putt when I saw the kid who picked up range balls coming along the fairway in an electric cart.

He was obviously coming from the clubhouse with a message. Since both doctors in the foursome were obstetricians, the chance of his having a message for me was remote. But I waited. I am not too sound on sidehill putts.

"Mr. Callahan," the kid called, "I have a message for you."

"What is it?" I asked.

He looked embarrassed. "It's, uh, personal."

It was my turn to look embarrassed, but mostly I was frightened. Personal could mean accident, personal could mean death, personal could only mean Jan, my wife.

It was Jan. "She's in jail," the boy told me quietly. "She wants you to come there right away."

I climbed into the cart. "Something came up," I called to the others. "Something important." What else could I say—that my wife was in jail? I was a new member.

We rode in silence for about fifty yards and then the kid opened up. "No need to be embarrassed, Mr. Callahan. We got a call from Judge Vaughan's wife, too."

That put Jan in select company. Lois Vaughan was our town's most admired woman worker for worthy causes. But what worthy cause could land both of them in the clink?

The San Valdesto County jail was high on a hill north of town, close to the general hospital. The parking lot was half-filled when I got there and more cars were coming in. I pulled the Mustang into a space at the far end—just as Judge Vaughan's Mercedes pulled into the adjoining space.

We both got out and he looked at me over the top of his car, a tall, portly and obviously irritated man. "Jan, too?" he asked me.

I nodded.

He shook his head. "Damn that woman! Recording for the blind, the Salvation Army, the Heart Fund, the Children's Home Society—that's not enough for Lois. She's got to get herself involved with those pukey militant punks, too."

"Punks?"

"Punks," he repeated. "The only thing those kids know is protest. The only work they can handle is carrying signs."

"CANA," I guessed.

He nodded. "What else? Let's go in and bail them out."

Citizens Against Nuclear Armageddon—CANA. The local paper had been giving them the front page for a week. Ground had been broken out at Point Mirage, two miles from where we stood, for a projected nuclear power plant. CANA protesters, most of them from the local campus of the state university, had been picketing the place.

Toward the entrance we walked, across the blacktop shimmering in the unclouded sun. "I had Doc Ellers down three holes with four to go," he told me, "and then *this*!"

How sad, how cruel, that Armageddon should interrupt anything as important as that.... I said nothing.

"What in hell is this world coming to?" he asked me.

*Armageddon?* "You got me, Alan," I said.

The waiting room was full of long benches; the

benches were about half-occupied. They looked like parents to me, solid-citizen types.

At the counter, Alan told the woman behind it, "I'd like to talk with Sheriff Clune."

"He's busy, sir," she said.

"Well, you run in and tell him Judge Vaughan is here and let him decide how busy he is."

She gave him the bureaucratic glazed look for about ten seconds. "One moment, sir," she said quietly, and went to a phone on a nearby desk. She was back in less than a minute. "He'll see you. His office is—"

"I know where it is," he told her. "Let's go, Brock."

Sheriff Clune was as tall and thick as Judge Vaughan, but more—well, more macho looking, all cop. He got up from his big desk in his big office as we entered. "Alan, what can I do for you?"

"You can release my wife in my custody."

"Lois?"

"She's the only wife I have. She was brought in with those CANA creeps."

Clune smiled. "You won't need me for that, Alan. Only about half a dozen are being held, and I'm sure Lois isn't one of them. She's probably waiting for you outside right now."

"I hope so," Vaughan said. "If she isn't, I'll be back." He went out, and slammed the door behind him.

Clune sighed, and looked at me.

"The Judge forgot to introduce me," I said. "My name is Callahan. My wife was probably in the same group. I'll go outside and look for her."

He frowned. "Callahan? Just one moment." He bent over his desk and went through some papers. "Is that Mrs. Brock Callahan?"

I nodded.

"This is a slightly different case," he explained. "Most of them were guilty of unlawful assembly, and we decided to forget it. But assaulting a police officer . . . ?"

"With what?" I asked. "What is he, a midget?"

"This is hardly a time for levity, Mr. Callahan. The officer is over at County General right now, having some stitches taken in his scalp. Evidently she hit him on the head with her sign."

"I see. Was it provoked or unprovoked assault?"

He stared at me. It was almost a glare.

"My wife," I said, "weighs one hundred and eleven pounds and is an extremely law-abiding woman. As a matter of fact, I don't think she's even had so much as a parking ticket."

"I'm sure the judge will take her record into account."

"Judge? She's being held for trial?"

"She is. Bail has been set at five thousand dollars.'"

I had no further words for him. I went out and slammed the door, as my predecessor had, and went back to the big waiting room.

And there (incident two, coincidence one) at the bail counter was Joe Puma.

"Callahan!" he said. "What the hell you doing in San Valdesto?"

"Living. And you?"

"Oh, some bail bonds, some divorce work, credit and security checks, whatever makes me a buck. Been up here two years." He paused. "You still handling bail bonds?"

I shook my head. "That's not why I'm here. I'm retired. Joe, I don't have much money on me, and my wife is being held on five thousand dollars bail. You take care of it, and I'll mail you a check for five hundred tonight. Unless you accept credit cards?"

He shook his head. "No need, Brock, baby. I trust you. Let's go over here and fill out the forms."

I sent him the check that night. So what did I owe him? It's hard to explain to a layman, but I'll try. We were peers, or had been. We had prowled the Los Angeles streets together, despised by police, scorned by citizens less honest and gutty than we were. We had to scramble for every dirty dollar, which meant we had to cut a corner now and then. Who doesn't? Let's just say he was my kind of bastard.

When the deputy brought Jan out, she was steaming. "Cossacks!" she screamed. "Storm troopers! Who's the head man around here?"

"Sheriff Clune," I told her. "I've just come from his office. Let's go home."

"Like hell! Where's his office?"

"Jan, please—"

She said, very evenly, "Wait in the car if you want to. I'll find his office."

I knew that mood. I said, "Follow me."

The door was ajar when we got there. Jan pushed it open. Sheriff Clune was behind his desk. He looked up, frowning.

My bride had regained her composure. She said with quiet dignity, "I think you should know, Sheriff, that not only did your deputy call me an obscene name, he threatened me with physical violence. Lois Vaughan will confirm that. I expect you to take appropriate disciplinary action."  .

Down the hall in silence, out to the parking lot.

"What was the obscene name?" I asked her.

"Spindleshanks."

I kept a straight face. "And the threat?"

"He said, 'You hit me with that sign, spindleshanks, and I'll break it over your pretty head.' "

"It's possible," I said doubtfully, "a clever defense attorney might make something out of that."

"We won't need an attorney. Did you notice how worried he looked when I mentioned Lois Vaughan?"

Nothing from me. I held the door of the Mustang open for her. She got in and I went around to climb behind the wheel.

"Are my legs really that thin?" she asked.

"They are thin, but very well proportioned. And you certainly have a pretty head, as the man said. I'm not sure we have a case."

"There'll be no case. I don't want to cook. Let's eat out."

"Okay."

"There's a CANA meeting at eight o'clock,"

she told me. "I think you should come with me. I think you should get involved in community affairs."

I didn't argue with her. She could do far worse than hitting me over the head with a sign. She could get one of her convenient headaches.

"I'll go," I said.

## 2

THE MEETING WAS HELD in the Odd Fellows' Hall, a properly named forum for the assemblage. They were a mixed group, both long- and short-haired students, a few militant firebrands, counterbalanced by the solid, stolid, older Citizens Who Care.

The firebrands ranted their noisy absurdities, studded with non sequiturs. The concerned senior citizens were more rational, but duller. Most of the students either sat and listened quietly or asked pertinent questions, a comforting thought for the future.

And then it was time for the adversary windup discussion, a geology professor from the university versus a representative from the South Coast Electric Company.

It was a mismatch, both orally and physically, a travesty.

The professor was a bull of a man with a voice like thunder who knew what he was talking about—or seemed to. The company man was thin as a matador, but his employer had given him a dull sword. He was plainly not a geologist, simply their front man. All he knew was what he read from his sheets on the lectern.

The bull bellowed about land shifts and land drifts, about earthquake faults and underground water erosion, and made it all as vivid and frightening as a horror story.

The matador read his dull statistics, his printed quotes from other alleged experts, all in his pedestrian voice as he sank deeper and deeper into the dust of the ring.

At the few bullfights I have witnessed, I have always rooted for the bull. Almost everybody in the room was rooting for the bull tonight. I would have put my money on him, but my heart belonged to the matador. Gutty losers are my spiritual twins.

Even at the end, during the question and answer period, his sword bent, his body gored in half a dozen places, my twin fought on, erect, defiant, proud.

As we filed out Jan said, "Professor Barlow certainly made a fool out of that company fink, didn't he?"

"The man is no fink. Mr. Hemingway named him years ago in a story called 'The Undefeated.' I forget his hero's name."

"You're crazy," she said. "The man is a fink. You do admire losers, don't you?"

"No, ma'am. I *sympathize* with losers. I reserve my admiration for people who don't quit."

"Macho, macho," she said. "Macho yo-yo, ex-jock macho yo-yo. How did I ever get tied up with you?"

"Any damned time you want to get untied, just say the word."

She stopped walking and gripped my arm. "Hey! What's the matter with you? I was joking!"

"I'm sorry," I said. "I—I overreacted. I apologize."

"You do that a lot lately," she said. "You need something more important than golf to occupy your mind. We could use you in CANA."

"Okay. I wonder how your Professor Barlow would fare against animals who run both ways?"

"You've lost me again," she said wearily. "What did you mean by that?"

"It's from a letter Hemingway wrote to William Faulkner. Faulkner had this collection of hunting stories out, and Mr. H wrote him that he would have admired them more if they'd dealt with animals that run both ways."

Nothing from her.

"You see, what he meant, lions and tigers run *toward* you at times, but deer and pheasants and rabbits—"

She said patiently, "I *know* what Hemingway meant. What I was thinking. . . I'm not sure you belong in CANA."

"I'll decide that," I said. "Are you getting a headache?"

"Of course not. I don't fight that way. Let's hurry home, lover."

SHE IS A GREAT GIRL, my Jan. Our attitudes rarely mesh, but she is a great girl. At breakfast I told her, "You are a great girl—or woman, if you prefer."

"I'm getting to an age where I prefer girl," she said. "Do you mean I'm great in the hay?"

"All around. I love you so much it hurts."

"It's mutual. Why do we fight so often?"

"Because we are what we are. If I could change you or you could change me, we would both be less than we are."

"That's either cornball or profound," she said. "I'll give it a lot of thought as I do my household chores."

"I have told you a dozen times that we can afford a housekeeper. Why don't you hire one?"

"When I can find one who isn't a slob, I'll hire one. Golf again today?"

"Nope. I think I'll run down and pay a vist to Lenny Devlin."

"Now that is a real nice thought. Give him my love."

Lenny "Pepper" Devlin had been my boyhood idol. He was a San Valdesto native, but had ventured out into the cruel world at fifteen to play third base in the Appalachian league. Two years later he was playing in the majors. When he reached forty-one, he put the glove in mothballs and came back to his hometown with his beloved Gloria. They had no kids; all they had was each other.

His Gloria had been killed in a car crash two years ago. Lenny had gone to the place where he now lived eight months ago.

On the way down I stopped at a liquor store to buy him a bottle of vintage corn and a carton of cigarettes. I know that cigarettes are a cancer-inducing agent, but Lenny already had that—what he called "The Big C." He still drank and he still smoked when the doctors weren't watching, and he would continue both until the final out.

The place where he lived was a converted mansion near the foothills. It was run by a wealthy woman who also had not been blessed with children. Some of the residents were sick, some were simply old. All, like Lenny, were dying. Who isn't?

He was in the backyard, sitting under a jacaranda, reading the sport pages of the *Los Angeles Times*.

"Brock the Rock," he said as I came over. "What's in the bag?"

"Opiates," I said. "How's it going, Pepper?"

"I'm still here."

In his playing days he had weighed a hundred and sixty-five pounds. He now weighed a hundred and ten. But he was still here, at the age of fifty-seven.

"Those damned Dodgers!" he said. "Every night they invent a new way to lose a ball game. They're inventors, that's what they are. They're not ballplayers, they're inventors."

"Right!" I took out a package of cigarettes, opened it, and handed him one.

"Any of those quacks around?" he asked me.

I shook my head. "It's Wednesday, Lenny. There's an AMA rule—all doctors are required to play golf every Wednesday. Except for psychiatrists. They play tennis.''

He nodded. ''I forgot. What's new with you?''

''Nothing exciting. Have you been reading about the CANA gang? Or do you only read the sports page?''

''I read everything,'' he said, ''including the obituaries. What about CANA?''

''I went to one of their meetings last night. There was a speaker there named Barlow. Isn't that a famous name in this town?''

''Hell, yes! They go back to the Spanish land grants. They owned a quarter of this country at one time. Which Barlow was it?''

''I forget his first name. He teaches geology out at U.C.S.V.''

''Judson,'' he said. ''I went to high school with him. He was a second-string fullback at Princeton. All the Barlow men went there.''

''He's a *big* man. I mean—physically.''

''And a big bully, and a big windbag. I got this feeling that if you gave him an enema, you could bury him in a matchbox.''

''That's the way I read him. What I can't figure, he's on the wrong side of the fence. He doesn't shape up as the environmentalist type.''

''If *he's* on the wrong side of the fence, there's an angle to it. You used to play cop; look for the hole in the fence.''

''I didn't *play* cop, Lenny. I was a state licensed and bonded private investigator. I worked at it.''

''Hurrah! What you were was the best damned

football player the Rams ever had. The rest was hogwash, and you know it."

"Take that back, Lenny," I warned him. "Or the bottle goes home with me."

"You brought a bottle? Buddy, compared with you, Sherlock Holmes was a bush-league rookie." He reached into a pocket of his robe and pulled out two small plastic cups. "I had a hunch you might drop in today. Let's drink to us."

We drank to us. We talked of better times and bigger men, under the shadow of the jacaranda. We talked until it was time for Lenny's nap. I helped him up the stairs and into bed. I put the bottle in the darkest corner of his closet and the cigarettes deep in his desk drawer, behind his stationery.

"Come back soon," he said sleepily.

"Sure thing. Hang in there, kid."

Out into the sun, out to my baking car. Some world. Heroes die and assholes flourish. . . .

Where now, and why? Point Mirage, maybe, to look over the battleground? If I was to be a soldier for CANA, it might be wise to check out the areas of strategic retreat.

I took the freeway to the Eucalyptus Lane turnoff and that all the way to the sea. There was no milling mob today, only four stalwart soldiers. They were two students, Lois Vaughan, and a small, weathered woman in a cotton dress and tennis shoes. No deputies were in sight, just a single uniformed company guard.

"Brock," Lois cried, "you've come to join us!"

"It's almost lunchtime," I said. "Why don't I take the four of you to lunch?"

She looked at my little car. "In that?"

"We could take your car."

We took her car, three tons of air-conditioned limousine. I thought of mentioning that monsters like it were a major reason why we had to search for new energy sources. But coming from a raw recruit that would seem like mutiny.

"Find a place that has martinis," she said. "It's been a hot, dry day."

On a bluff overlooking the ocean we found a place with a sign that proclaimed booze was served. The kids and I ordered draft beer, Lois a martini. The old girl in the tennis shoes ordered a double boilermaker.

"Small army today," I said. "People losing interest?"

"We're putting on a big show tomorrow," she explained. "The governor is coming down from Sacramento."

"Huh!" the taller kid said. "Old Wishy-washy is trying to make Brownie points."

Lois stared at him.

"He's not on our side," the boy said. "And while I'm on the subject, if South Coast had sent a geologist to that meeting last night, old Barlow would have been cut to ribbons. I never heard so much nonsense. He sounded desperate to me. He's not *that* bad a geologist."

"Professor Barlow," Lois said primly, "has been one of our biggest contributors. I resent that kind of talk."

The kid said nothing, staring at his beer.

"I don't resent it," I said. "What did you mean by desperate?"

"I mean he said things that would be laughed at by any first-semester geology major. He sounded as if stopping the construction of that power plant meant more to him than his professional sense of ethics or honesty."

"You think Point Mirage is a safe place to put the plant?"

"I don't think, with our limited knowledge of nuclear power producing, there's a safe place for it anywhere in the world. But if I were to pick the safest place in Southern California, Point Mirage would be my choice."

"That's your major, geology?"

He nodded. "As it was for my father and grandfather. Luckily for our cause, there were no other geology students at the meeting last night."

Lois took a deep breath, looked at me, and then at the boilermaker lady. "I, uh, don't know what to say. Professor Barlow is an old friend of my husband's and has supported our cause since its inception." She looked at me. "Could I have another martini?"

"Coming up," I said.

"And another boilermaker for me," the other lady said, "but make it a single this time. Lois, I haven't spoken up until now, but I've been wondering how a Barlow could be on *our* side. I've lived here and fought here all my life, but this is the first time I've ever had a Barlow on my side. It just doesn't figure."

"And what can we do about it?"

"Tell him to keep sending in the loot and keep his big mouth shut. The way I see it, any ally in a fight is a good ally."

The kids laughed. Lois sighed.

"I second the motion," I said. "Show of hands?"

We all raised our hands—and finally Lois did, too.

The students had classes after lunch, Lois a PTA meeting, and the old girl had to get back to her ranch. Which left only one soldier on the firing line.

Back and forth I walked in the hot sun, carrying a sign that read Say No to Nuclear Nihilism, while the guard yawned in the shade of his shack.

I felt foolish. Noble, but still foolish.

**3**

RIDING HOME, I dreamed up a new name for the bull: "Fifth Column Barlow." Lenny had told me the Barlows had once owned a quarter of the county. Would that possibly include the six acres of shoreline property that the power plant occupied? Had the Barlows sold the property to South Coast Electric and later discovered there was oil on it? Or realized that California coastal property had tripled in value in the last couple of years? Was there possibly a clause in the contract that stated the property would revert to its original owners if some outside agency prevented the plant from being built?

That is the pattern I dreamed up on the ride home. It might not make sense, but investigating it would be more interesting than playing golf every day. I hadn't been the world's most successful investigator, but my record there was more respectable than I had ever achieved on the fairways of this state.

Jan, too, has her patterns. "Where the hell have you been?" she asked me. "I was expecting you for lunch."

"I had lunch with your good friend Lois Vaughan."

"A four-hour lunch? Where did you eat it, in bed?"

"In bed— Jan, Lois must weigh one hundred and sixty pounds!"

"Oh? You mean you only commit adultery with thin women?"

Very quietly and very calmly I said, "I have just spent three hours walking in that hot sun. Why don't you get us a pair of cool tall drinks and I'll explain it all."

"All right. With booze in them, I suppose?"

"Vodka and tonic would be nice."

I sat in the air-conditioned dimness of the den, listening to the clink of ice dropping into glasses in the kitchen. She couldn't be as absurdly jealous as she is, I thought, if she didn't love me. I hoped she would always be jealous.

She came in, handed me my drink, and sat down across from me in a higher chair, like a judge on his bench.

"Your Honor," I said, "it was like this. . . ." and went on to tell her the story of my day. "And now," I finished, "if you want to confirm my story, you can phone Lois and she can give you the names of those students and that woman rancher and you can call them and then you can apologize."

"I apologize now," she said. "How was Lenny?"

"A little weaker. Not much."

"I suppose you brought him cigarettes and whiskey again."

"I did. I think a man has a right to die any damned way he wants to."

"I'm sure you do. Do you realize, if he's getting sedatives, whiskey could be poison to him?"

"Lenny doesn't take sedatives. He went through half a season at Pittsburgh playing with two broken fingers."

"He would. The invictus kid."

"A soul brother," I said. "What do you think about that student's critique of Barlow's performance last night?"

She shrugged. "What do I know about geology? I suppose this will give you an excuse to drop out of CANA?"

"Would I have carried that dumb sign for three hours if I were going to desert the cause? My duty, as I see it, is to use my impressive investigative skills to clear the professor's good name."

She looked at me suspiciously. "You must have had more than one drink at that lunch."

"I had one beer," I said, "while Lois sat there soaking up martinis. I could use another vodka and tonic right now."

"Okay," she said. "I guess I could, too."

WE WERE WATCHING "Barney Miller" on the tube when the phone rang. I was the nearest to the den doorway; I went into the kitchen to answer it.

A woman's voice said, "You don't know me, Mr. Callahan. I'm Ellen Puma, Joe's wife. He told me at dinner last night that he had seen you yesterday afternoon. I wondered if you were working on a case together."

"No. I'm retired. Is there something wrong?"

"He went out after dinner last night and I haven't seen him since."

"Did he say where he was going?"

"To meet somebody. He didn't tell me any more than that."

"I think you had better call the police," I suggested.

A silence from her end.

"I know," I said. "Joe doesn't want the police in his business. I had a few battles with them myself when I was active."

"He got along with the police in Los Angeles," she said. "It's been different up here. I don't know what to do. Do you think he could be working on something dangerous? Maybe he had to go out of town."

"It's possible. I still think you should call the police."

"Do you happen to know any—any decent ones down there?"

"I know one, a friend of mine, but he doesn't work nights. I'll call him at home. Has this ever happened before?"

"Once," she said, "three years ago. And I still don't know what that case was about. I suppose it could be the same this time. I'd appreciate it if you'd call your friend."

"I will. Right now."

Lieutenant Bernard Vogel answered the phone himself. "Bernie," I said, "this is Brock."

"It would be," he said sourly. "Right in the middle of 'Barney Miller.' What's on your mind?"

"Joe Puma's wife just phoned me. Do you know Joe?"

"I know the bum, a real shoddy operator out of smogtown. Is *he* a friend of yours?"

"For a couple of minutes, would you pretend you're not a cop? Would you pretend you're a human being? Joe Puma is no angel, I'll grant you, but I've known a dozen cops who were worse."

"Name one," he said.

"Oh, drop dead!" I said, and hung up.

I didn't leave the phone. When he called back, fifteen seconds later, he said, "So the man's a friend of yours. He must be better than I rated him. What happened?"

"He's missing. He hasn't been home since dinnertime last night."

"Why didn't his wife phone the police station?"

"She might get one of my dirty dozen. I promised her I'd phone one I trusted and your name immediately leaped to the front of my mind."

"Okay, I'll call Captain Dahl. He's working tonight. When are we going to play poker again?"

"As soon as I finish this book I'm reading. It's called *Percentages for Proper Play*. Thanks, buddy."

"You're welcome, sucker. I'll call Dahl as soon as 'Barney Miller' is over."

When I came back to the den, Jan asked, "Who was that?"

"The first call was from Joe Puma's wife. The second, Bernie Vogel's return call."

"Who is Joe Puma?"

"He's the man who bailed you out of the clink yesterday. His wife said he's been missing since last night. So I called Bernie, and he got snotty and I hung up and he called back. What happened while I was gone?"

"You know what happened. This is a rerun. Why do you always have to fight with everybody? Even sweet Bernie!"

*Sweet* Bernie? I had no answer for that one.

"I remember," she said. "You explained it to me this morning. Because they are they and you are you and if they could change you or you could change them, you would all be less than you are."

"That's roughly it," I said. "I'm going to take a shower."

The warm water came down, caressing me, washing away the grime of three sweaty hours of dusty plodding in the sun.

Joe, Joe, Joe.... The private investigators in this town were little more than camera buffs. They took pictures of accident scenes for insurance claimants, of cracked sidewalks in front of public buildings where some citizen had fallen and needed evidence for a suit. They did credit and security checks and—as Joe had said—a few divorces.

They didn't handle bail bonds or go out into the dark night to meet a—

A what? A client? Certainly not to meet anybody dangerous, not Joe. He watched TV too much; he saw what happened to those nitwits, always getting knocked in the head. Any sensible investigator who got knocked in the head as often as those private eyes on the tube did would have to realize he was in a business he didn't understand.

"A shoddy operator out of smogtown," that's what Vogel had called Joe. Bernie should work the Los Angeles scene for a couple of years and learn a new definition of shoddy.

Why was I dreaming up a scenario for Joe Puma? For all I knew he was curled up with some cozy blonde in a local motel. For that, maybe, Joe would go out into the dark night.

In our comfortable home in Montevista, a suburb of San Valdesto, I slept a dreamless sleep, ninety miles from the mean streets of smogtown.

At breakfast Jan said, "Our governor's in town. And where do you think he spent the night?"

"I can't wait to hear."

"At the home of Professor Judson Barlow."

"Wishy-washy and the bull, strange bedfellows," I said.

"Would you clarify that?"

"It's what the students called our governor, 'Wishy-washy.' I think of Barlow as the bull. Politics makes strange bedfellows."

"You still don't like him, do you? But yesterday you said you were going to— How did you word it? Oh, you were going to use your impressive investigative skills to clear the professor's good name."

"You have an exceptional memory," I said. "How come you forgot I don't like salt on my eggs?"

She looked at her eggs. "I gave you the wrong plate." She handed hers over and took mine. "You were lying yesterday, weren't you?"

"Not about Lois. About the bull, maybe a little. But now he has slept with Wishy-washy. He's probably a big contributor to Wishy's campaign fund."

"I hope so. Wouldn't that be good for CANA?"

I didn't have time to answer. The phone rang and she went to answer it. When she came back she said, "That was Lois. All charges against me have been dropped."

"How nice to have friends with clout," I said. "Did she ask for me?"

It was her turn to get cheated out of a reply. The phone rang again. I went this time. It was Vogel. "We found Puma. We found him dead. He was shot."

"Jesus!"

"I'm over at his house," Vogel went on. "Maybe you'd better get over here. His wife is hysterical. She could use a friend." He gave me the address.

I told Jan, "Joe Puma has been killed. I'm going over to his house."

I was halfway to the bedroom for my car keys and my wallet when she asked, "How did it happen?"

"I don't know. I'll phone you if I'm going to be late."

Joe Puma's house was a pink stucco California standard in a stucco tract. The Bermuda-grass lawn was gray, the blacktop driveway cracked and pitted. Two uniformed officers were standing on the walk in front.

I had met one of them, but had forgotten his name. "Callahan!" he said. "What're you doing here?"

"Vogel phoned me. What happened?"

He shrugged. "I've only been here a couple of minutes."

The other man said, "Some cheap peeper went and got himself shot. If I remember right, he had a Mafia connection down in L.A."

"You're full of shit," I said.

"Hey!" he growled, and took half a step toward me.

The other officer stepped between us. "Easy, George. Callahan used to be a shamus, too."

"That figures," the other man said.

"Go right in, Brock," my semifriend said. "Vogel's in there."

The front door opened directly into the living room. A thin bleached-blond woman sat on a worn davenport at the far end, staring down at the floor. Vogel stood a few feet from her, his notebook in his hand.

When the woman looked up I said, "I'm Brock Callahan."

"Thank you for coming," she said. "We—don't have many friends in town."

Vogel said, "Well, I guess that's as much as you can tell me. Could I have that key now?"

She got up and left the room.

"What key?" I asked Vogel.

"The key to his office. There might be a lead in his files."

"Wouldn't you call that an invasion of privacy? Maybe Mrs. Puma needs a lawyer."

"Brock, the man is dead! We don't plan to bring him to trial on anything we might find in his files."

"The department might get some juicy publicity out of them, though."

"Watch it!"

Ellen Puma came in with the key as we glared at each other. She said, "It's all right, Mr. Callahan. The lieutenant explained why he wanted it," She handed him the key. "I apologize for all those crazy things I said about the police. I must have been hysterical."

"You had a right to be," he said. "I want to talk with you outside, Brock."

Outside on the gray lawn he asked, "What's with you? If you were forty pounds lighter, I would have belted you in there."

"I'm sorry. I walked in steamed." I pointed at the uniformed men. "That lard ass on the right made a crack about Joe being mixed up with the Mafia."

"So? Didn't he work with Scarlatti? Isn't Scarlatti a big wheel in the mob?"

"Scarlatti's son," I explained patiently, "was kidnapped. The kidnappers sure as hell didn't want one of his hoodlums to act as intermediary. They asked for Puma. Would they ask for Joe if they thought he was in the mob?''

"I don't know and you don't know. But you should know me well enough by now to know I don't leak juicy items to the press.''

"I'll say it again. I'm sorry.''

"Okay. But you walk carefully on this. This is police business.''

"Yes, sir. I'll be careful, sir.''

He went over to the uniformed men. I went back into the house.

Mrs. Puma was sitting on the couch again. "Don't worry about that key,'' she told me. "All Joe kept down there was meaningless stuff. I know, because I was his secretary his first year in town. His important files are here. Even I don't know what's in them.''

"Why didn't you tell the police that?''

"It wouldn't matter to me what they found there,'' she said, "but we have a son. If Joe didn't want me to know what was in there, I figure he wouldn't want Joey to know.''

I said, "I'm sure there's nothing there that would shock me. Joe and I walked the same dirty streets. Are the papers locked up?''

She nodded. "And I don't have the key. But it's only a one-drawer file. You could—'' She broke off. "What am I talking about? You're not going to get mixed up in this. Just because Joe was down there bailing out Joey and happened to run into you—''

"Bailing out Joey? What did he do?''

"Nothing serious. He didn't even need bail. He was picketing out at that CANA protest at Point Mirage, and they hauled him in, along with about fifty of the others." (Incident three, coincidence two.)

I asked, "Where's Joey now?"

"He was running in that track meet down in Ventura. I finally got in touch with him. He's on his way home now. I want to thank you for dropping in."

"I'll see you again," I said. "Is that file cabinet light enough for me to carry to the car?"

# 4

SHE WAS CRYING, and before I left she started to tremble. I said, "I could wait with you until Joey gets here."

She shook her head. "I'm not going to break down again. That's over with. But you—I mean— why should you waste your time? Joe's dead. Does it matter if we know who killed him? How can that matter, compared with knowing that he's dead?"

It was a question that I had often asked myself. I didn't give her the answer I had arrived at— vindictive retribution. I said, "Maybe it will save somebody else. As for wasting my time, I've been doing that for three months."

"It could be dangerous," she said. "You don't even carry a gun, do you? Joe didn't."

"That's TV bilge," I told her. "None of us carry guns. Let me put it this way; I don't want the bastard who shot him to get away with it."

She wiped her eyes with a tissue, and blew her nose. "I suppose you know I can't pay you."

"I wouldn't take the money if you could. This is personal." Personal is a much nicer word than vindictive. I asked, "Is there a doorway to the garage the neighbors can't see? I don't want any of them telling the police they saw me take a file cabinet out of here.''

"There's a doorway from the kitchen," she told me.

I drove my car into the garage and pulled down the overhead door. I carried the file out and put it into the trunk. I told her, "There might not be anything in there that can help us. I want you to think back on this past week. Try to remember everything Joe talked with you about.'' I paused. "Tell Joey to do the same."

She nodded. "Thank you, Brock. And bless you.''

I was charged up more than a decent man should have been on the drive home. I was back on the prowl, hunting an animal who ran both ways.

*Does a man have to die to make you whole, you cheap peeper? Don't try to give it moral over- tones. Don't call it justice or some noble knight's crusade. You enjoy the hunt.*

At home Jan asked, "What happened? I mean—how did it happen?''

"He was shot. His body was found in his car on a lot behind a deserted gas station out on Arroyo Road.''

"Do the police know when he was shot?''

"Not yet, probably. I didn't talk with them much. Mrs. Puma told me what little I know.''

"You'd better have lunch," she said. "We're due at the rally at two o'clock.''

I thought of the cabinet in the car. I had

planned to open that this afternoon. But I didn't want to give Jan further grounds for her suspicion that I didn't belong in CANA.

THE RALLY was not out at the plant site; it was held at the California league baseball park in town. I don't know what the original name of the place was, but it had been renamed Lenny Devlin Field when the town's most notable athlete had come home to die.

There would be short speeches by proponents of both sides before our many-sided governor would unleash his homilies.

The company was represented by a geologist today. CANA by a local citizen who had to be a statistician by trade. He had all the frightening figures.

These are the things I learned: Nuclear power provided less than five percent of California's energy supply. *Routine* releases of radioactive gas had been proven to cause leukemia, cancer and genetic mutations. Wind-blown plutonium from the Rocky Flats nuclear plant was associated with a one-hundred-percent increase in various forms of cancer in the population downwind from the plant. And on and on....

The man made me proud I had carried that dumb sign.

And then it was the company geologist's turn. "Two nights ago," he told us, "I was scheduled to appear here at your meeting to debate the geological safety of the Point Mirage site. Due to an attack of the twenty-four hour flu, I was unable to appear. Unfortunately, the gentleman who replaced me, Stuart Engelke from our legal department, has no background in geology." He paused. "Which your Professor Judson Barlow realized. However, we took the liberty of taping that meeting, and the tape has been sent to Boulder, to the Geological Society there. The absurd statements made by Professor Barlow at that meeting are a discredit to the man and his profession. Let me assure you this is *not* only a company view of it; any competent geologist will agree with what I've just told you. The media representatives here might suggest to the governor that he reexamine the credentials of any state university professor who—"

He never had a chance to finish. The boos poured down, the signs began to wave wildly, two tomatoes and one egg narrowly missed him. He stood there, as erect and defiant as his matador associate had, neither flinching nor ducking.

"Let's get out of here," I said to Jan. "They're not going to let him finish. And my stomach isn't strong enough to listen to the governor."

"Five minutes?" Jan asked. "I want to hear if the governor's on our side."

The governor's good friend, his host in town, had just been demeaned in front of this crowd. If there was a shred of loyalty in the man, now would be the time to show it.

But there was no anger in his voice, and no defense of his friend. He opened with his standard two-handed speech. On the one hand we must consider this, but on the other hand . . . .

I remembered from my youth that President Truman had suffered the same problem with his economic advisers. Old Harry had announced that what this country needed was a one-armed economist.

"That student was right about him," I told Jan. "He's not on our side. Let's go."

She looked at me suspiciously. "You've been champing to leave ever since we got here. Where do you plan to go?"

"Well, I—promised Mrs. Puma I'd do a few errands for her. Her and her boy—"

"Go," she said. "I'll get a ride home with Lois."

I didn't go home nor over to the Puma house. I drove out to Arroyo Road, to visit the scene of the crime, as the newspapers love to call it.

It was a meandering road, roughly following the bends of the dry streambed that ran along its northern edge. At the far ocean end of it there were some sumptuous estates. At the beginning end, off Harvest Avenue, it was mostly avocado groves and deserted agricultural plots waiting for the spread of the city to make their owners rich.

The station had to be a relic of the 1930s, a small shack of imitation adobe blocks with a corrugated iron roof. A faded lopsided sign hanging by one hook near the doorway offered ethyl gasoline at six gallons for one dollar.

On the weed-filled gravel parking lot behind it, the remnants of a rust-eroded Model A Ford coupe body was lying on its side. A thin gray cat sat in the shade of the car, studying me carefully.

There was no house close enough to cause its occupants alarm at the sound of a shot in the night. I couldn't believe Joe had been this dumb, meeting somebody with a gun in a spot as isolated as this. Joe had his faults, but stupidity hadn't been one of them. The fact that he was found here, of course, didn't automatically mean he had died here. The police would check that out.

The police, ah, yes, the police. . . . Here I was, at the scene of the crime, with some files they didn't know about in the trunk of my car. The gray cat hadn't moved, watching me warily.

It was still watching me when I drove away, heading for the Puma home.

A young man with his father's blunt face and his mother's thin figure opened the door to my ring.

"Joey?" I asked.

He nodded.

"I'm Brock Callahan. I was here this morning."

"I know. Mom told me. Come in. She's—resting. I'll get her."

"No need," I said. "I just wondered if your father had a copying machine."

He nodded again. "An old Xerox, but it works pretty well. It's in the utility room."

"I've been worrying about that file cabinet I carted away this morning. If the police should find out I have it, we could all be in a lot of trouble."

"We sure as hell wouldn't tell them."

"But they could find out. So I thought I would copy the papers I need, and take them with me.

But I'm not very good at picking locks, and if I pry it open, and they find it that way—''

''I know where the key is,'' he said. ''You'd better drive into the garage.''

He was waiting inside when I drove into the garage. He helped me carry the file cabinet into the utility room. There he reached under the soaking tub and brought out a key.

I handed him the papers one by one; he ran the machine. There weren't many papers in this small cabinet, about fifty. Some of them simply notebook-size lined sheets with phone numbers and addresses on them.

When he'd finished, we put the original papers back and the cabinet back in its original resting place.

''Want to talk for a few minutes?'' I asked him.

''Sure. Could you use a beer? Pop always kept a six-pack in the fridge.''

''I know. It was his favorite beverage. I'd appreciate one.''

''We could sit in the backyard,'' he said. ''It's cooler out there and we won't disturb mom.''

The backyard was fenced with six-foot redwood boards, its borders bright with flowers of all the colors that bloom in May. We sat on the steps of the utility-room porch.

''Track man?'' I asked him.

''Right. The four-forty and the half mile. But you don't get track scholarships in law school. Goodbye law school.''

I said nothing.

''About a week ago,'' he went on, ''pop told me

it was in the bag. He told me not to tell mom, but he was on a case that would earn him thirty grand."

"Thirty thousand dollars! For an investigation? Didn't that seem strange to you?"

"It sure did. And not telling mom? But I didn't question him. I didn't give a damn, I guess. Maybe, if I had—" His voice broke.

"Easy, Joey," I said quietly. "It could have been perfectly legitimate."

"Oh, yes! But don't tell mom."

"That doesn't have to mean it was crooked. If it was dangerous, he wouldn't want her to know, either, would he?"

"Mr. Callahan, I'm not a baby. At a hundred and twenty dollars a day, plus expenses, thirty thousand dollars in one week is not a fee, it's a payoff."

"Not always. Some clients pay by the job, some by the day. And there's bounty money, too. Let's not jump to conclusions."

"Okay, okay. Mom said you were going to work on—on this."

"I plan to."

"We appreciate it," he said. "Pop always said you were the greatest."

"Well," I said modestly, "there are a few pretty sharp investigators I could name you who—"

"He didn't mean investigator," Joey told me. "He meant the greatest lineman the Rams ever had."

# 5

JAN WAS IN THE DEN when I got home, nursing a martini on the rocks and watching an educational TV show on the Mayan civilization. She had been trying to improve her mind the last couple of months. Boredom, I guess.

"Any violence at the rally after I left?" I asked her. "Or did our friends run out of tomatoes?"

"That's not funny," she said. "It's cheaply cynical. What are those papers?"

"I picked them up at Puma's house. Did the paper come?"

She gestured toward the coffee table where the local evening paper was still folded. "Brock, you're not going to get involved in that murder, are you?"

"Not seriously. But if I can learn anything that would help the police—"

"You're lying," she said. "I'm not going to argue with you, but I don't like it." She looked at her empty glass. "I wonder if I should have another? We'll be drinking at the Vaughans'—"

"The Vaughans'?"

"Have you forgotten? We're going there for a buffet dinner. Mostly CANA people."

"Alan will love that."

"Alan better not complain too much. You don't think the Vaughans could live the way they do on a judge's salary, do you?"

"So that's the picture. *She* has the money. I was wondering why he would marry such a fat woman."

"Stop it!"

"You need another drink," I said soothingly. "Make me one while you're up, and then we'll compare our afternoons."

She went out to get more ice cubes. I picked up the paper.

Joe had made the front page, a full-column story with three pictures. One picture was of Joe, one of the gas station, and one of his car on the lot behind it.

He had been shot with a .32 caliber weapon in the right eye at close range. So far as the coroner could determine, he had died on the night before last between midnight and two o'clock. The car had been seen on the lot by several passersby since that time, but none had reported it. A prowl-car officer had discovered it after receiving the missing-person report.

Joe was identified as a private investigator who had moved up here two years ago and become active in community affairs, including Rotary and the American Legion. There was no mention of his part in the Scarlatti kidnapping. There would be no funeral. He had belonged to the local memorial society and his prearranged choice of cremation would be handled by them.

Jan brought me my drink. "I couldn't read about it. It would remind me of the risks you used to take."

"Honey, for all we know, Joe was killed by a jealous husband."

"You mean he was that kind of man? That isn't the picture I got from you."

I didn't argue with her. Jan wouldn't think of wearing a dress that was two months out of style, but her sexual attitudes were seventeenth-century Puritan.

It had been an orderly rally, she told me, mollified by our governor. He had promised in his quiet and apparently sensible way that both sides of this very serious controversy would be studied by him, after consultation with both environmental and scientific experts. However, he had pointed out, if we had all been more careful with our use of the available energy supply, this dangerous search for alternatives could have been avoided.

"I guess he meant until he is president," Jan said. "He's a fink!"

She had voted for him and I hadn't. I didn't point this out.

"And now," she said, "what have you been doing since you deserted me?"

I told her most of it, all except the part about my having had the file cabinet in my car and having the papers Xeroxed.

"Thirty thousand dollars?" she said. "Maybe he wasn't an adulterer. Maybe he was only a blackmailer."

I shrugged. "I'm going to take a shower."

THE VAUGHAN ESTATE was high in the hills above Montevista. It could be called a home, but four manicured acres made it an estate to me.

The parking lot was half-filled with cars when we got there, most of them small and foreign. These earnest young people who were trying to save America made their major purchases abroad.

Though the buffet was set up in the back, on the patio overlooking the pool, the clatter of conversation could be heard long before we reached the front door.

"Yakety yakety-yak!" Jan said. "Everybody talking, nobody listening."

"Don't be a summer soldier," I said. "We can leave early."

The young people were jammed around the buffet tables, the older citizens in small groups, drinking. Lois took Jan away to introduce her to somebody she "just had to meet"; her husband told me: "Grab those two chairs down by the shade garden. I'll bring you a drink. Bourbon, isn't it, bourbon and water?"

"That's it. Light on the water."

He must have had a hot round today and he was going to tell me about it stroke by stroke.

I had guessed right. I listened patiently, uttering an admiring ejaculation from time to time, feigning great interest all the way to the fourteen-foot downhill putt on the eighteenth green that had earned him his impressive seventy-nine.

"Congratulations," I said. "That was some round!"

"Thanks. Another drink?"

"I could use one. I had to go to that rally to-day."

"I know what you mean. I'll be right back."

When he brought it, I said, "The governor surprised me. That company geologist really raked his good friend and host over the coals, and got no word of defense from the governor."

He sat down and sipped his drink. "Lois told me about it. Maybe His Honor got wind of Judson's interest in the Trinity Investment Company."

"What's that?"

"I'm not too clear on it. The lawyers around town refer to it as 'the unholy trinity.' There's some hoodlum front money in it, I guess. They own that property that surrounds the plant. The way I hear it, they were planning to build a luxury housing development there with six tennis courts and an eighteen-hole golf course."

"Did Barlow own the land originally?"

He nodded. "You know, Jud and I used to be pretty close friends. But lately—" He shook his head.

I smiled. "He's lost you *and* the governor, huh?"

"He's lost me. He and the governor were classmates at Princeton. They've been friends for a long time. Jud poured plenty of money into his campaigns. But no politician can afford to be linked to the syndicate." He paused. "At least, not publicly."

"And not too many luxury-home buyers would

want to live near a nuclear power plant, would they?''

"You've got the picture," he said. "Maybe we'd better get something to eat before those hippies clean out all the tables."

We left early, as I'd promised Jan. Our phone was ringing when we opened the front door.

I got to it in time. It was Vogel. "I've been calling you for three hours. Where the hell have you been?''

"I had a kilo of heroin to deliver," I told him, "and the buyer kept haggling over the price. Why do you ask?''

"Because I got a couple calls from Puma's neighbors. They said you drove into his garage twice today. Why?''

"That's where I store the heroin. What makes it police business?''

"I made it clear to you this morning that this case *is* our business. What were you hauling out of there?''

"Lieutenant, are we friends or aren't we?''

"We are. But you're crowding it, Brock."

"So are you. My business with Mrs. Puma and her son is personal.''

"I'll ask you once more. What were you hauling?''

"Good night, Bernie," I said, and hung up.

He didn't call back. He would sleep on it. He would cool off. He had to make noises like a cop to protect his pension, but way down deep he trusted me. We were friends.

"There's nothing but garbage on the tube," Jan said. "I think I'll read."

"Me, too," I said.

She read her book in the den; I took the Puma reports to the dining-room table where I could spread them out.

There were names and addresses and phone numbers for some clients, and a hodgepodge of scattered names, numbers and addresses that only Joe would understand. There were records of payments and their dates.

One name jumped off the page—Mrs. Stuart Engelke. That had to be the matador's wife. How many Stuart Engelkes were there in this town, or any town?

Another coincidence. . . . If there was a pattern here, it would need a mind more complex than mine to find a line of inquiry in it.

Mrs. Stuart Engelke had paid Joe Puma $263.40. Would that mean two days of work and $23.40 in expenses?

When a wife is the client, it's usually divorce work. Maybe Mrs. Engelke had made a two-day check of her husband's movements and found him innocent. I hoped so. I still admired that man, even if he was on the wrong side of the CANA controversy.

These, Ellen Puma had told me, were Joe's important cases. A two-day divorce investigation didn't seem to belong in that category. The records of those would be in his office file along with the credit and security checks. That was the file the police probably had custody of by now.

So far as I could tell from Joe's hieroglyphics, this was the only divorce case in his home file. These would be the cases where Joe walked that thin line between the legal and the illegal, and occasionally stepped over it.

It was eleven o'clock now, too late to phone Vogel at home. I would phone him at the station tomorrow. I would buy him an expensive lunch.

# 6

I PHONED HIM after breakfast. "Lunch at Pierre's?" he said. "You paying for it?"

"Unless you want to."

"I don't. What do you think you can buy with a fancy lunch?"

"Your forgiveness. I was rude to you last night."

"I see. And now you've decided to tell me what you hauled out of Puma's garage?"

"We can talk about it. I'm willing to cooperate."

"Cooperation is a two-way street. This Puma business is a one-way street and *we're* on it."

"Okay. But Pierre has fresh sole today. Sole amandine and a bottle of Château Lavigne Blanc?"

He sighed. "One o'clock?"

"One o'clock at Pierre's. Wear a tie."

When I came back to the breakfast room for another cup of coffee, Jan said, "There's a piece in the *Times* about the murder." She handed me the paper.

The *Los Angeles Times* had given it less ink than the local papers, but they had included an

account of Joe's part in the Scarlatti kidnapping.
The F.B.I. had taken a very dim view of his role
in that. Paying off kidnappers without Bureau
participation, they believed, rarely led to the ap-
prehension of the kidnappers. So did paying
them off *with* their participation, but they didn't
publish those statistics.

"Who were you talking to?" Jan asked.

"Bernie. I apologized to him for my rudeness of
last night. I'm taking him to lunch."

"And getting involved in his business?"

"I doubt it. He was definite about that. But it
could have a peripheral connection to our CANA
war and—"

"You're lying," she interrupted. "What possible connection could there be?"

"Well, Joe's kid is one of our soldiers, and
there are some other angles I'm not at liberty to
discuss."

"You're not at liberty to discuss with your
wife?"

I shook my head. "I'm sorry, honey. Only with
the police. But if you want me to desert CANA
and go back to golf—"

"You're a phony," she said.

"Why don't you ask Lois what her husband
told me last night?" I said patiently. "Ask her to
tell you about the Trinity Investment Company."

"You tell me."

"Not me. I'm a phony. Ask your good friend.
And now it's time to go to work." I went back to
the dining room and the Puma papers.

There were four seven-digit numbers on one

note-sized sheet of paper with nothing but letters after them. They could be the initials of people or some code of Joe's.

I picked one that had the letters L.K. after it and dialed the number on the phone.

"The Kendfelt residence," a female voice answered.

"Could I speak with Mr. Kendfelt please?"

"Mr. Oren or Mr. Lowell?"

"Lowell," I said.

"I'm sorry. He's not at home. Could he call you back?"

"I'm leaving the house now. I'll phone him back later."

There was, I discovered, no Kendfelt in the phone book. These were probably all unlisted numbers. I would check the other three, in time.

The rest of it was still only a collection of names and numbers. Eventually maybe at least some of them would have meaning.

VOGEL HELD HIS GLASS of wine up to the light and admired it. "What did you drink," he asked me, "before your uncle died and made you rich?"

"Same as you, beer and cheap bourbon."

"I drink Scotch," he informed me. "The cheap bourbon is in my house for guests who don't appreciate real whiskey. What's on your mind?"

"I was wondering if you'd learned anything at Joe's office."

"Nothing that has given us a lead—yet. We had his files for about an hour before the Feds came and asked for them."

"The F.B.I.?"

He shook his head. "Criminal Division of the Justice Department."

"Why?"

"You tell me. He was your friend."

"You mean they didn't explain why they wanted the files?"

"Those boys? They don't explain *anything*. Arrogant bastards!"

"And you just turned them over without a fight?"

"We turned over copies—and charged them for them. And now it's your turn."

I had planned to tell him the whole truth. I could work with him. But the Feds? I told him a truth that wasn't whole. I said, "Joe had a one-drawer file at home. I put it in the trunk of my car. I never opened that trunk again until I brought the file back."

He sipped his wine. "I lied to you last night. It wasn't the neighbors who reported your two trips to Puma's. It was the Feds."

"They're watching his house?"

"They must be."

I said, "They'll probably get a court order to check any records he might have there."

Bernie shook his head. "I doubt it. They're pussyfooting on this one. Very hush-hush. What I told you could get me into trouble. For the record, *I* didn't tell you."

I nodded.

"What was in the files, Brock?"

"I never took them out of the car until I brought them back!"

"I heard you the first time. What was in them?"

"Don't try to trap me, Bernie. You've probably got them already."

"Nope. And we're not going to. At least for a while. Under orders from the chief."

"Do you want them? I mean personally. Joe's kid trusts me and so does his wife. And I trust you. If I ask them, they'll give them to me. We'll go over there together as soon as we're through eating. Fair enough?"

"Fair enough," he said.

We ate for a while in silence, and then I said, "Joe do much divorce work? This should be a profitable town for it."

"Maybe a third of what I saw seemed to be. That really must be a crummy way to make a living, prowling around, prying into a man's sex life."

"Or a woman's. It's not any crummier than making porno movies, or working on the vice squad. A little more wine? Maybe a split?"

"A split should do it. It goes great with this sole."

"You order it," I said. "I'll phone to see if the Pumas are home."

"Don't bother," he said. "I'm not going over there. I was only testing you."

I had guessed he was. I said, "Those Justice Department boys are now running the show, huh?"

"Order the wine and shut up," he said.

"Bernie," I said quietly. "Joe was murdered. Murder is not a federal crime. Didn't the chief point that out to those Washington hotshots?"

"The justice department," he said stiffly, "is not going to impede our investigation of your friend's murder." He beckoned to a waiter and pointed at the bottle of wine. "Another split, please?"

When the waiter went away, I said, "They're not going to impede mine, either. You can tell them that."

"You tell 'em," he said. "I'm sick of arguing with you. You're rich enough to post your own bail. You don't have Puma for that anymore."

"That was in the files, too?"

He nodded. "And they have a copy. I'm going to enjoy this, Callahan finally getting his lumps. I hope you're not an easy bleeder."

"I'm shaking with fright."

"Not now," he said. "But maybe later."

I am not one of those eyes who keeps looking in the rearview mirror to see if some evil person is following me. But when Bernie and I had parted—friends again—on Pierre's parking lot, I happened to notice this yellow Pinto hatchback with a Yosemite sticker on the windshield. There was a man sitting behind the wheel.

Then, because I was only a couple of blocks from his place, I decided to stop in and see Lenny.

As I walked up the steps to the porch of the converted mansion, I saw another yellow Pinto hatchback pull into the space behind my car. There are a lot of those models in town, but how many with a Yosemite sticker on the windshield?

The lady who ran the place told me Lenny was taking a nap and she thought he should get his sleep. He'd had a bad morning.

"Tell him I was here," I said. "Tell him I'll be back soon."

"I certainly will. He enjoys your visits so much!"

"Would it be all right," I asked her, "if I went out through the backyard? It's a shortcut to a friend's house."

"Of course," she said. "I hope it's not another sick friend?"

"Not yet," I said.

Through the yard to the alley, down the alley to the front of her house again. The driver of the Pinto, a tall, thin man in bureacratic blue, left his car and walked up the steps of the house. I waited at the foot of the steps.

It must have been at least five minutes before he reappeared. He saw me when he came out onto the porch. He stood there, staring down at me.

"Looking for me?" I asked him.

"I don't know what you're talking about," he said. "I was visiting a friend."

I went up the steps. "Let's go in and ask the lady if you were visiting a friend." I gripped him by the elbow. "Come on."

He jerked his arm away. "Who the hell do you think you are?"

"We both know that. Let's go in and find out if you're a liar."

"Mr. Callahan," he said in a voice he tried to make ominous, "I strongly advise you to drop the subject. I'm not looking for trouble and you'd be wise not to make any."

"Mr. X," I said, "if I ever catch you tailing me again, you are going to wind up with a lot less teeth than you now have."

He took a breath. "I think you had better come down to police headquarters with me and get this straightened out."

"Only if you're a policeman. If you're not, it's already straightened out. Good day to you, sir."

I turned my back on him and went down the steps to my car. He was still standing on the porch when I drove away.

So far as I could judge, the Engelke investigation was the only divorce case in Joe's home file. According to Vogel, they made up a third of the files in his office. It was possible that Mrs. Engelke's concern had not been adultery.

How could I ask her? Let me count the ways. . . .

I remembered the address, 6300 Calle Cortez, in the foothills on the north end of town. That was an expensive section. Stuart Engelke couldn't earn that kind of money from the South Coast Electric Company, unless he owned it. Maybe, like Judge Alan Vaughan, he had married it.

The house was one of the older homes in the section, with an acre of formal garden in front through which the green concrete driveway curved to the canopied entrance. The architecture was Spanish, or maybe Moorish, with a red-tile roof and wrought-iron grillwork adorning the narrow windows.

The woman who answered the door had raven-black hair and large brown eyes and an olive skin. Her figure was full, but only an ultra-outré dress designer would consider it heavy.

"Mrs. Engelke?" I asked.

She nodded.

"My name is Brock Callahan. I'm on the Professional Ethics Committee of the California Association of Private Investigators. There have been some client complaints registered with us about a former member named Joseph Puma. He—"

"Isn't he the man who was murdered?" she asked.

I nodded. "Unfortunately, because of what I consider to be absurdly outdated Association rules, his widow's pension will be substantially diminished unless—"

"Come in," she said.

I came into an entry hall not much longer than the Holland Tunnel. An archway to the right opened into an immense living room, an archway to the left into a smaller, dimmer room, where she led me.

"Drink?" she asked, pointing to a small portable bar.

I was about to decline, until I saw the bottle of Wild Turkey. "Bourbon and water would suit me fine," I said.

She poured me a big jolt, added some water, and poured one for herself without the water. She dropped the ice cubes in and brought the drinks over to where I stood.

"Sit down," she said. "I've been waiting for an excuse for a drink all afternoon."

"Me, too," I said.

I sat in a large leather chair. She sat on a hassock across from me. She said, "Mr. Puma's services were entirely satisfactory to me. Do the police have any idea of who killed him?"

"I don't know. They don't confide in me."

She sipped her drink. "I had my husband followed for two days. I am a very jealous woman, Mr. Callahan, and my husband is a very handsome man." She smiled. "Mr. Puma not only found my suspicions groundless, he gave me a fatherly lecture when he finished his report."

"I've always thought of Joe as a solid family man," I said.

"I'm sure he is. Are you Jan Callahan's husband?"

I nodded. "Do you know Jan?"

"I met her once. At Lois Vaughan's. Lois used to call me as a fill-in occasionally for her regular bridge group. But now that she's so active in CANA—" She sighed. "My husband works for the South Coast Electric Company."

"That's an unfortunate situation," I said. "It's strained a lot of relationships in town."

"Oh, yes! Lois is not the only friend who's dropped us. I had the impression from your wife, Mr. Callahan, that you were retired."

"I am. But I'm on the advisory board of the association and because I live here they asked me to check out these complaints."

"I'm sure," she said, "you'll find Mr. Puma as innocent as he found my husband to be. You won't be questioning my husband about this, will you?"

I shook my head.

She smiled. "It will be our secret. Another drink?"

"I'm sorry," I said, and stood up. "I really love that Wild Turkey. But I'm due home at four. And I, too, Mrs. Engelke, have a jealous wife."

# 7

JAN WAS WATCHING the educational channel
again, a program devoted to the fine art of basket
weaving.

"Do you remember a Mrs. Engelke?" I asked
her.

"I think so. Was she at the three-hour lunch
you had with Bernie?"

"No. She's the wife of the man who debated
Professor Barlow."

"I remember her. She used to substitute at
Lois's bridge. Beautiful woman. A little heavy
for your taste, I imagine. Where did you see
her?"

"At her house. She was a client of Joe Puma's.
That, of course, I shouldn't have told you and
you must never repeat. She paid Joe to follow
her husband."

"That silly man? She thought that mouse was
cheating on her?"

"Jan, please! The adversary is not *always* the
enemy!"

"Maybe not to jocks. Who else was with you in
Mrs. Engelke's house?"

"Oh, shut up!" I said.

She stared at me.

"A man has been murdered," I said, "and you sit there talking like some high-school pom-pom girl. What the hell difference does it make who else was in Mrs. Engelke's house?"

She went over to turn off the TV. "Would you like a drink?"

"It's only four o'clock. It's too early to drink."

"All right," she said quietly. "Then we'll sit here and you can tell me about your day."

I gave it to her, blow by blow, deleting only the Wild Turkey.

"You threatened a government officer?"

"I don't know. He didn't identify himself. I assumed he was. Now everything I have told you is strictly secret. And that includes Lois."

"Lois? What connection could she have with Joe Puma?"

"None. But Judson Barlow could, and possibly some others working in CANA."

"I'm not following you."

I told her what Judge Vaughan had told me about Barlow's dubious associates in the Trinity Investment Company. "So now," I went on, "we have a real clean professional-type killing, a bullet through the eye. We also have the coincidence of a South Coast Electric Company employee making Joe's important file, probably the only adultery investigation in that file. Why?"

"I don't know."

"Neither do I. His wife said it was only a two-day investigation. Then why was it in that file and why is the justice department interested?"

"That was the only adultery investigation in the file?"

"I think so. I'm not sure—yet."

"You're building a theory on nothing, maybe?"

"So far, yes. To tell you the truth, I'm walking around in a fog."

"I know it's a trivial question," she told me, "but did Mrs. Engelke find out? Was her husband cheating on her?"

"He was as clean as the driven snow," I said, "just like your husband."

"I remember that old joke," she said. "He was as clean as the driven snow, but he drifted. Is it time for a drink now?"

"I'll get them," I said, "as an apology for telling you to shut up."

"I'll get them," she said. "I had it coming. Whiskey?"

The half glass of 101-proof Wild Turkey was still warm in my stomach. I said, "Bring me a bottle of Einlicher. I had too much wine at lunch."

I nursed my beer. She nibbled at her martini. "Back to the wars," she said. "You can't quit working, can you?"

"Joe Puma was a friend of mine."

"A *close* friend? Joe? You know he wasn't."

"I hate killers."

"And enjoy the hunt," she added.

I sipped my beer. *Home is the hunter, home from the hills. . . .* Our doorbell chimed.

"You answer it," I said. "It's probably the Feds."

She made no move. I got up and went to the door.

It was Bernie. "Is it the cocktail hour," he asked me, "and do you have drinkable Scotch?"

"Yes, to both questions. Come in and say hello to Jan."

In the cool, dim den, Jan said, "It's been too long a time, Bernie. Is Brock your only friend in this family?"

"I prefer your company," he said. "But your husband has set up camp in my hair."

"How do you like your Scotch?" I asked him.

"In a glass," he said. "How else? No ice, no water."

"You sound grumpy."

"Run and get the booze," he said, "and then we'll talk."

"If it's business," Jan said, "maybe I'd better leave."

He smiled at her. "Why? With his big mouth, I'm sure he doesn't have any secrets you don't share."

"Sit down," I said, "and cool off. I'll get your drink."

I brought it to him and sat down across from him. He said, "It's been a hectic day downtown. What do you two know about CANA?"

Jan said, "I've been working with them for three weeks. Brock joined the cause a couple of days ago. I'm proud to be associated with them."

"But you don't know much about them?"

"I respect the people I've been working with. I didn't put them through a security check, if that's what you mean."

"And the Trinity Investment Company?"

"You'd have to ask Brock about that."

He looked at me.

I said, "All I know is what Judge Vaughan told me. And all he'd heard were rumors. The attorneys around town, he told me, call it 'the unholy trinity.' I understand Judson Barlow is one of the partners in it. The land they planned to develop that surrounds the power plant is all original Barlow property."

"But why should the governor want to know about it? A couple of men from his staff were questioning everybody but the meter maids down at the station."

"The governor," I said, "has a very sensitive political antenna. Judson Barlow is one of his big-money contributors."

He nodded. "I see. This is great Scotch."

"Thank you. Another?"

He shook his head. "Now, how about this G-man you threatened? What was that all about?"

"If you mean the unidentified man who followed me from Pierre's to the place where I told him off, I didn't know he was a Fed because he didn't tell me he was."

"He followed you from Pierre's? Then he must have been the man who told the chief we had lunch together."

"Probably. Did the chief read you the riot act?"

"He did."

"So, he's a politician, too."

"It has nothing to do with politics. It's you. He doesn't like you."

"I would be very uncomfortable if he did. I'm not his kind of people. And neither are you, Bernie."

He took a deep breath. "The arrogance of the rich!"

"He was *always* arrogant," Jan said, "even before he was rich. But he's still a good man to have on your side, Bernie."

"I know," he said wearily. "I know. If I didn't know that, he'd be in the slammer right now."

For the second time that day, we parted friends. I hadn't told him about my visit to Mrs. Engelke. He is also a cop, subject to the high-level pressures of politicians and the people who buy politicians.

After dinner I asked Jan, "Do we have any important social engagements this evening?"

She shook her head.

"Then I think I'll run over and see the Pumas. Do you want to go along?"

She shook her head again.

"It'll only be an hour or so. Mrs. Puma told me they don't have many friends in town."

"Go," she said. "Don't forget your Junior G-man badge."

The wind had shifted; it was a cool night. On the freeway below, the campers and the vans and the trailers were heading for the open spaces, bringing nuclear energy closer every minute.

Wastrels, all of us, a spoiled tribe of over-indulged children concerned only with *now* and *mine*.

There were cars parked in the street along the Puma block, but none of them was occupied. Joey opened the door to my ring.

"Hi!" he said. "Something to tell us?"

I shook my head. "Just thought I'd drop in."

"Mom's in the kitchen. Want a cup of coffee?"

"I'd like one."

From a narrow breakfast nook at the far end of the kitchen, Ellen Puma looked up and smiled. "Did Joey tell you the news we got today?"

"I didn't have time," he said. "Pop bought an insurance policy three weeks ago. One of those monthly term policies for twenty thousand dollars."

"Now Joey can go to law school," Mrs. Puma said.

"Good," I said. "And how about you?"

"I'll get along. I spent twelve years as a legal secretary. I can find work. Sit down and have a cup of coffee."

Her blond hair was pulled straight back, her face devoid of makeup. A pioneer mother in a twentieth-century tract house.

Joey brought me a cup of coffee and slid in next to his mother on the bench opposite me. She said, "Now tell him the other news, Joey."

"They picked up the files in that cabinet," he said.

"Federal officers?"

"One was. There was a uniformed cop with him. I didn't argue with them."

"Why would the F.B.I. be interested in Joe's files?" his mother asked.

I didn't correct her. I said, "Who knows? Maybe they still resent his part in the Scarlatti kidnapping. They can be petulant."

"I can't believe that," she said. "It must be something else."

I shrugged. "Do you plan to stay up here or go back to Los Angeles?"

"I'm staying. It's not a bad town. Los Angeles is just too—too busy for me. And Joey likes it here."

Some more small talk over the coffee.... When I left, Joey walked to the car with me.

"That was no F.B.I. agent, was it? That was just for mom, that kidnapping bit."

"Yes."

"I thought they might find out about the cabinet here," he said. "They won't learn anything from those files."

"Why not?"

"Pop had some boxes of old files stored in the garage. I took the papers out of the cabinet and put some old ones in."

"Why?"

"Because I don't want them to find out about the thirty thousand dollars. If they find out, mom will."

"You're only guessing that it was dirty money."

"Mr. Callahan, you were in the same business. What's your guess?"

"I don't have any," I lied. "That was a foolish thing you did, Joey, hiding evidence. You could be in a lot of trouble."

"I don't see how. They asked for the papers that were in the cabinet when they got there. We turned them over. Did you tell them about the cabinet?"

"No. But I told a cop friend about it. He must have told them. They're better equipped to find your father's killer than I am. Don't you want to know who killed your father?"

"It's not important. The important thing is he's *dead*!" He started to cry.

I stood there, saying nothing. He had held up well through this so far. He needed tears.

When he was under control again, I said, "I'll keep in touch. You holler if you need any help with the estate, or anything."

I waited until he had gone back to the house and closed the door before driving away.

Joe, the reformed horse player, had hedged his thirty-thousand-dollar bet with an insurance policy, the cheapest he could buy. One way or another, Joey was going to become a lawyer. Joe must have thought that was a more honorable trade. Joe had been naive in some ways.

The boob tube was silent; Jan was reading again.

"Nothing on the education channel?" I asked her.

"Guitar lessons," she said. "How are the Pumas holding up?"

"They're making it." I told her about the insurance policy.

"He bought it three weeks ago? Is that a clue?"

"I don't know. I'll be in the dining room trying to make some sense out of these files. Maybe, later, we could have some cocoa?"

"When this book bogs down," she said. "I'll bring you some."

## 8

WE NEVER GOT TO THE COCOA. The night nurse at Lenny's place phoned to tell me Lenny was weakening. "I can't make out what he's saying, but he keeps mentioning your name. You're the only visitor he has, Mr. Callahan."

"I'll be right down," I said.

"What was that?" Jan asked.

"The nurse at Lenny's place."

She stared at me. "He's not—"

"He's not dead. Not yet. Do you want to go along?"

She shook her head. "I couldn't take it. Will you tell him that?"

I nodded. "He'll understand."

They had given him a standing ovation when he had driven in the winning run in the '51 series. He had been a Rookie of the Year, M.V.P. twice and six times a Golden Glover. In his native town they had named a park after him.

But now? *You're the only visitor he has, Mr. Callahan.* If man is made in God's image, I'm not sure I want to meet Him.

The room was dim, hardly more than a nightlight. "Brock?" he asked. "Is that you, buddy?"

"It is." I went over to hold his bone-thin hand. "Jan couldn't come."

"Jan who?" he asked. His voice was hoarse. "I know why they called you The Rock. You are. Thy name is Peter and on this rock I build my church."

"You want a priest, Lenny?"

"Hell, no. I want a drink. Did you bring one?"

"I didn't have time. Is there some left in that bottle in the closet?"

"Look," he said.

I looked. There were a couple of ounces left. I put it in a water glass and held it to his lips. His final communion. He dribbled some. I wiped his mouth with the back of my hand.

"I saw The Man," he told me.

"What man?"

"The guy with the scythe."

"No. It's those drugs they give you, Pepper. You saw what wasn't there."

"He's here. You win some, you lose some. But nobody wins the big one, right? Nobody beats The Man."

"He's *not* here. If he was, I'd have seen him."

"Don't argue, Brock. Just sit a while."

I was still holding his hand when the doctor came in. I was still holding it when the doctor said, "He's dead."

Lenny's ghost had been in the room. My ghost was on the sidewalk below when I went out, his yellow Pinto parked at the curb behind him.

"I want to talk to you, Callahan," he said.

"Not now." I went down the steps and started to go around him.

"Now, you arrogant bastard," he said. "I'm a federal officer." He grabbed my arm, hard enough to hurt.

The shot I gave him would have put down a lesser man. I caught him with a looping right hand between his neck and his chin. He bounced off his Pinto and came back with a haymaker of his own. It nailed me below my right eye.

I tried to smash the top of my head into his face. But he twisted his head to one side and we started grappling. We were alternating the grappling with some stiff shots below the belt when the wail of the siren was heard in the night and the red light came flashing down the street.

Captain Dahl was in charge of the night watch. He and the Fed went into the captain's office while I sat on a bench in the hall, the indignant taxpayer. I sat and sat and sat.

Eventually the chief came bustling down the hall from the street doorway. Dahl must have phoned him at home. He glared at me as he went past and into Dahl's office, slamming the door behind him.

The door opened again in a few minutes and Dahl beckoned to me.

The chief was standing next to Dahl's desk. The Fed sat in a chair on the other side of it. A roly-poly man, Chief Chandler Harris, ornery, political, but fairly honest.

"Assaulting a federal officer," he grated. "Do you know what that can get you?"

"Six days in Hawaii and a ten-speed bicycle on a game show if I guess right. How was I to know he was a federal officer?"

"Didn't he tell you he was?"

"He told me. He didn't prove it. If some yo-yo walks up to me on the street, grabs my arm so it hurts, and tells me he's Peter Pan, what do I do—fly away with him?"

The Fed said, "He knows who I am."

"Like hell I do! Tell me your name. I may want to look you up later."

"Oh, Christ!" Harris said. "Let's all sit down and cool off."

We all sat down, I on a bench again near the door.

"Your version first," Harris said.

I gave it to him from the phone call to the sidewalk encounter.

He stared at me. "Lenny's dead?"

I nodded.

He looked at the Fed. "Lenny Devlin is one of our local—well, I guess you'd say idols. I can understand why Mr. Callahan would be disturbed." He looked at me. "You were close to him, weren't you, Brock?"

I had gone from a glare to Mr. Callahan to Brock. My stock was rising. I said, "Somebody had to be. A man shouldn't die alone in a town where he's idolized."

The chief's red face grew a touch redder.

Dahl said, "I was planning to go and see him."

"What for?" I asked. "To question him?"

"Watch your goddamned tongue, peeper," he growled.

I started to get up.

"Sit down!" Harris said. "And you, Captain, you cool it."

The Fed said, "I don't intend to press charges."

"I do," I said, "as soon as I learn your name. I intend to find out why you've been harassing me and my attorney agrees I should. Maybe we can find out in court."

A silence. Chief Harris sighed and looked questioningly at the Fed. The Fed gave Harris his blank bureaucratic glazed gaze. Nothing from him beyond that.

Harris said, "There will be no charges filed on either side."

"That's my decision to make, not yours."

"Oh, Jesus! What do you want from us?"

"I want Mr. X over there to stop following me. I want to keep looking for the bastard who killed Joe Puma."

"We're looking for him. You want to work with us, is that it?"

"If you insist. I'm not sure Bernie Vogel would be happy about that. He told me to keep my damned nose out of it."

"He told you that because I told him to tell you that. You and Bernie are friends, aren't you?"

"Most of the time."

"Okay. You work it out with him. And you keep *nothing* from him. Is that understood?"

"Yes, sir."

I nodded at Dahl, glared at Mr. X, said, "Good night," and went out.

I could mourn Lenny but I couldn't regret his death. It had been a long time coming. He had expected it. Maybe Joe had, too—or why the insurance policy? Why, why, why.... This mess was full of whys.

Jan was waiting at the door when I got home. "What happened? I phoned down there and the nurse told me you had left more than hour before I called. Where have you been?"

"Talking with Chief Harris and Captain Dahl and a G-man."

"I see. Which one blackened your eye?"

"I don't want to talk about it tonight."

"Would you like your cocoa now?"

"Some whiskey. Lenny's dead.'

"I know. The nurse told me. You go sit down and relax. I'll get your drink."

She knew that a drink and a soft chair would loosen my tongue. I recounted the night's adventure.

When I'd finished she said, "You're still down there, aren't you?"

"Down where?"

"In Los Angeles, in that chintzy little office, playing Hawkshaw. It was your living then. Why do you need it now?"

"Because it's all I know, except for football. I'm a little too old for football. But I'm too damned young to retire. Only a slob would retire at my age. I have to do *something*, Jan!"

"Okay, okay," she said wearily. "Is your eye the only place that you hurt?"

"No. He gave me some mean shots in the groin. Want to see?"

"Not tonight," she said. "I have a headache."

## 9

MY NIGHTS HAD BEEN FILLED with dreams lately.
Tonight's was crazier than usual. Engelke was in
the Super Bowl, a quarterback. I kept trying to
tell him he didn't belong there; he was a matador, not a quarterback.

Nine years with the Rams, but never in the
Super Bowl. They had made it, finally, after I
had retired. In the dream I sat with Mrs. Engelke
in a VIP box, eating hot dogs and drinking Wild
Turkey.

In the morning, over the waffles, I said to my
bride, "This is a real stuffy town, isn't it? Are all
stuffy people cruel?"

"Here we go again," she said. "What brought
this on?"

"The Engelkes. That CANA business has made
them social pariahs."

"It's news to me. I'm not that social."

"I thought we could have some people in, you
know, the Vaughans and like that and—"

"I'd better clear it with Lois first. There might
be another reason why she dropped Nadia Engelke from her favored-persons list."

"I'll bet Judge Vaughan would prefer Stuart

Engelke to his old friend Professor Barlow."

"Possibly. But Alan doesn't make those decisions."

It was only a little after eight o'clock; Bernie would still be home. I phoned him there. "Chief Harris wants me to help you on the Puma case," I told him.

"It's too early in the day for low comedy," he said sourly. "When did you start drinking in the morning?"

"I'll meet you down at the station," I said, "after you've talked with Harris." I hung up.

When the phone rang, I told Jan, "That's Bernie. Tell him I'm in the shower."

"You're not in the shower *now*! Why do you insist on baiting that nice man?"

"It maintains our adversary relationship," I explained. "He'll understand."

The warm water caressed me. Nadia, what a beautiful name... Russian, probably. An olive-skinned Russian? Maybe her mother had been an Indian princess.

I had thought last night that my threat of taking the Fed to court and blowing his cover had been the reason for Harris letting me work with Bernie. Another thought came to me as I dressed. Maybe Bernie wouldn't be my ally. He might be playing watchdog for the department. What I might learn on my own they could funnel to the Feds through him.

I decided to bring them something they didn't know. Among Joe's papers still littering the dining-room table the most innocuous seemed to be the unlisted number I had already phoned, the home of Lowell and Oren Kendfelt. I scribbled the number on a piece of scrap paper.

Vogel was in his office when I got there. He looked at my discolored eye and smiled. "I warned you about getting your lumps from the Feds. You'll never learn, will you?"

"You should see the other guy."

"I've seen him, tall and skinny. Just wait until you run into their heavyweights."

I put the slip of paper on his desk. "I found this next to Joe's phone at his house. It must be an unlisted number. I called it. Somebody named Kendfelt, Oren and Lowell Kendfelt. Anybody you know?"

"I know Lowell. I arrested him years ago."

"For what?"

"For soliciting me in a gay bar."

"What the hell were you doing in a gay bar?"

"Waiting for him to solicit me."

"Entrapment? You?"

"Look, it wasn't my idea. I had my orders. Are we going to get along or aren't we?"

"I intend to try. Should I check this out?"

He stood up. "I'm going out to talk with a man on Arroyo Road. We'll stop at Kendfelt's on the way."

My morning's suspicion was strengthening, he was being too cooperative. Prove to me I'm wrong, Bernie, baby. Prove you're not as devious as I am.

We found the Kendfelt address in the city directory. It was an older home in a section of well-kept older homes only a few blocks beyond the business district. The other houses were Spanish or California stucco; Kendfelt's was red brick with white trim and white Colonial shutters.

The man who opened the door to our ring was tall and pale, with light golden hair and brilliant blue eyes. "Well, Sergeant Vogel! What have I done now?"

"Nothing I know of, Mr. Kendfelt. I've made lieutenant since last we met. I'm not here to harass you."

"In that case, you may come in," he said.

We came through a small foyer to a living room of hooked rugs and maple furniture, with Currier and Ives prints on the walls. A shorter, darker man rose from his chair as we entered.

"This is my friend Oren," Lowell said. "He took my surname when we decided to live together."

"Good morning, gentlemen," Oren said.

It was the voice I had heard on the phone, the voice I had thought was female.

Vogel said, "I—we're investigating the murder of a private investigator named Joseph Puma. He had your unlisted telephone number in his house and we wondered why."

"Because he was trying to blackmail me. However, Oren and I were up in San Francisco the night he was killed. I can supply you with the names of a dozen people who will attest to that."

"I'm sure there will be no need." Vogel said.

"And you don't have to answer this if you don't want to. But why did he think he had grounds for blackmail?"

Lowell smiled. "Can't you guess, Lieutenant? It was several months ago. I was about to become vice-president of Mr. Grundeman's little bank in Montevista. Do you know Mr. Grundeman?"

Vogel nodded. "I know the man. He's still living in the nineteenth century. I get the picture. So?"

"So rather than pay blackmail, I simply resigned."

"How much money did Puma want?"

"A thousand dollars. Which I could have paid. It was the principle involved—don't you see?"

"I do. Thanks for your cooperation."

Outside, Vogel asked, "What do you think of your friend now?"

"Kendfelt could be lying. Joe wouldn't risk an extortion rap for a lousy grand."

"A thousand here, a thousand there—?"

Could eventually get him enough to send Joey to law school.... I asked, "Where next? Arroyo Road?"

He nodded. "There's an old guy out there who might have a story to tell. It's probably nothing. Maybe he won't even talk to us. We got our lead from a bartender."

"He was sounding off in a bar?"

"Right." He pulled away from the curb and headed for Main Street. "You want to name those dozen cops who are worse than Joe Puma now?"

"Lay off, Bernie. Joe was hustling for every buck, trying to get his kid into law school—but this I can't believe. It was just as hard for me to believe you'd entrap a homosexual."

"That was my job. I was ordered to do it."

"You could have quit your job."

"I have to eat."

"So did Joe."

He drove down Main Street toward the freeway. "It's not the same and you know it. Let's drop the subject."

Silence in the city traffic, silence on the freeway. A quarter mile short of the Arroyo Road turnoff, he said, "Why do you pretend to be so moral? You don't even go to Mass anymore."

I laughed. "I'm not a saint and don't pretend to be. I apologize for making you feel guilty."

"Aagh—shut up!" he said.

"Yes, sir."

The old man who lived on Arroyo Road was an ornery old man. His ramshackle hut was about three blocks beyond the parking lot where Joe had died.

His first name was Calvin. I never learned his last name. Not that day. He was out on his gravel driveway, working on an ancient Plymouth, when we drove up.

He stood next to it, a wrench in his hand, as we walked toward him. "Oh, Christ, you—" he said to Vogel. "I ain't got enough trouble with this heap?"

"Relax, Calvin. I'm not bringing trouble."

"Fuzz is trouble," he said. "Fuzz is always trouble. Trouble's all you guys know."

"Thanks to people like you. I told you to relax. We're investigating that murder down the road. We have reason to believe you might be able to help us."

He looked between us—and smiled. "For how much?"

"Free."

"I don't know a damned thing. So long, boys." He bent over his engine again.

Vogel said, "You may have got the wrong idea of what a real prison is like from all your nights in the drunk tank. But impeding a murder investigation puts you in another league."

"I always wanted to make the majors," he said. "Goodbye, Loot."

"If I go, you go with me, Calvin."

He straightened up. "Okay. Let's go."

Vogel glared at him. I said, "How much?"

"We don't pay for information," Vogel said stiffly.

"I do."

Calvin smiled again. "I had a feeling you weren't a cop when you walked up. The way I figure it, this clunker needs new points, a new condenser and maybe a new distributor cap. Maybe sixteen, seventeen bucks?"

I handed him a twenty. "Keep the change and start talking."

"The way it was," he said, "I was coming back

from Barney's. You know—that bar down next to the railroad trestle?''

I nodded.

''I was walking. It was about two o'clock. I thought I'd cut across the field. It's shorter. Then I saw this car parked behind the filling station. It sure looked like a deserted car to me. I mean—it had to be, right? Unless there was some lovers in it.''

''That makes sense,'' I agreed.

''So if it's deserted, I'm not stealing, right? A Chrysler product it looked like in the dark. Maybe I could get the parts I needed.''

''And some parts you could sell,'' Vogel said.

Calvin looked at me and sighed. ''*Cops*—huh, buddy?''

''Go on,'' I said.

''Well, I'm still in the high grass over there when I see this other car pull off the road and into the lot. Great big black job. Two guys got out and went over to open the front door of the parked car. The inside lights went on when they opened the door and I could see this guy sitting there.'' He took a deep breath.

''And they shot him?''

''Nah. There was no shot. I think the guy was already dead.''

''Did you notice the license number of the black car?''

''Hell, no. I wasn't interested. I did notice it was a Nevada license, though. I used to live in Nevada. They went back to the road after a couple of minutes and really burned rubber.''

"Which way did they go on Arroyo Road?"

He pointed toward the ocean.

Vogel asked, "Do you think you could identify those two men?"

Calvin shook his head. "Their faces were never in the light. So help me, that's the gospel truth."

"Thanks," I said.

"Glad to help," he said. "If you're going toward town, could you give me a lift to that auto-parts store next to Barney's? I can walk back."

"If you keep your greasy hands off the upholstery," Vogel said.

Calvin sighed once more. "Cops!"

We dropped him off at Payless Auto Parts and continued toward town. Vogel asked, "You know who lives in that swanky section at the ocean end of Arroyo Road?"

"I know a few people. I suppose you mean Tony Romolo?"

"That's the man. Since his old man went to the clink, Tony took over the family. Did they ever get along with the Scarlattis? Never. And your buddy worked for Vincent Scarlatti."

"One time. Only on the kidnapping."

"So far as you know. Nevada license plates. No wonder the Feds are in town. Let them handle it."

"Sure. Why should we care who gets killed in our town?"

"Drop dead. Are you going to take me to Pierre's for lunch?"

"Not today. I have to see somebody."

"Not alone. Not if it has anything to do with this case."

"It doesn't," I lied. "I'm also working for CANA, remember."

"Okay. Don't call me. I'll call you."

A thought hit me. "Bernie, you said 'No wonder the Feds are in town.' Don't you know why they are?"

He shook his head. "Not even Chief Harris knows that."

**10**

IF THE NEVADA MEN had been heading out of town they had traveled in the wrong direction. Arroyo Road ended at the residential area along the ocean. It was the only road in or out of the area.

I left my car in the police station parking lot and walked over to the South Coast Electric Company building on Main Street.

Stuart Engelke's office was on the second floor. In the outer office, a buxom, middle-aged woman was typing at a desk near the door. She looked up as I came in.

"My name is Brock Callahan," I told her. "Is Mr. Engelke busy?"

"Do you have an appointment?"

I shook my head.

"Could you tell me the nature of—" She paused to smile. "I mean, you're not selling anything, are you?"

"No. It's kind of dumb. I've been working with CANA, you see, but lately I've been wondering—"

She smiled again. "I'm sure he'll see you." She picked up her phone, pressed a button, waited a

few seconds and said, "A Mr. Brock Callahan to
see you." Then, to me, "Go right in, Mr. Callahan."

He was standing behind his desk when I
entered. "Brock Callahan? I know that name."

"Through my wife, maybe? She knows your
wife."

"Are you joking? Brock Callahan? You and
Merlin Olsen—immortals! And neither of you
ever in a Super Bowl. It's criminal!"

"I'm sold," I said. "Goodbye, CANA."

"That's why you're here?"

I nodded. "My wife had me working with
them. But lately—I don't know. I mean, that
Trinity Investment Company, and all—"

He gestured toward a chair. "Sit down, Brock,
and we'll talk."

We sat down, an immortal and his fan. He
asked, "Where did you hear about the Trinity Investment Company?"

"From Judge Vaughan. He didn't know much
about it. Some of the attorneys around town
have hinted there might be some syndicate
money in it."

"Our attorneys have the same feeling about
them. I guess the governor's people are beginning to suspect it, too. Were you at the rally?"

"Until about halfway through the governor's
speech."

"Oh, yes. First the one hand and then the
other. He could make a living as a juggler."

"And this Judson Barlow," I said. "That was
his land, wasn't it? And there have been some

rumors around town about his recent connections.''

He nodded. ''Mafia. But only peripheral, so far as we know now. Didn't you work as a private investigator after you retired?''

''For a while. And then my uncle died and I came up here from Los Angeles to lead the good life.''

He smiled. ''We could use a competent investigator. But you don't need the money, I suppose.''

''I do a little work around town. Never for pay. This is the kind of mess that intrigues me.''

His phone buzzed. He picked it up. ''Send her right in,'' he said. ''Tell her she is about to meet my idol.''

We were both standing when she came in, Nadia Engelke. She stood in the doorway, glaring at me. ''You liar! You blabbermouth! You promised me, you weasel!''

''Nadia!'' Engelke said. ''For God's sake, have you gone crazy? What's this all about?''

She closed the door and looked between us doubtfully.

Engelke said, ''I have to assume you two have met. Would it be presumptuous of me to ask where?''

Great lines. I stifled my laugh.

''I—'' she said. ''I— Oh, damn it!''

''You had me followed again,'' he said. ''You had Brock Callahan spy on me?''

She shook her head. ''Joseph Puma. That man who was murdered.''

"And now we're both embarrassed," he said. "And I'm sure Mr. Callahan is, too. Oh, Nadia—"

"I'm not embarrassed," I said. "And I can understand her reaction. There have been a few coincidences in this Puma business. This happens to be one of the more unfortunate ones."

Engelke's face was rigid. "My wife, Brock, has this absurd notion that I married her for her money. She—"

"I don't want to hear any more," I interrupted. "There's been embarrassment enough. Why don't we all go out for lunch and talk things out?"

"And let Nadia pay for it," he said. "She has the money."

"Mr. Engelke," I told him, "that was a rotten thing to say."

He nodded. "It was, and I apologize. Call me Stu." He went over to hug his wife.

At the restaurant I gave him my Ethics Committee Story and we went on to other topics.

He told me the company had thought of hiring a local investigator but none of them seemed qualified. "Mr. Puma," he went on, "was the most qualified local man—until we checked his background."

"And the name Scarlatti jumped up and hit you in the eye?"

"To put it graphically."

"So far as I know, Joe acted solely as an intermediary in that kidnapping. Why did you need an investigator?"

"We discussed that in my office."

"The Trinity outfit?"

He nodded. "And one of our company attorneys told me yesterday that there are government officers in town interested in the Puma murder. We might have hired a double agent."

"You mean Joe might have been working for Trinity?"

He shrugged. "Who knows? Let's talk about football."

"I'd rather talk about CANA. Will Barlow get his land back if the power plant doesn't go through?"

"Yes. At the price he paid for it years ago. And he can build his luxury subdivision without having to worry about buyers who might be scared away if the plant was there."

"So that's why he made a fool of himself in your debate."

"Most people thought I was the fool that night." •

"You were bad," I said. "But you were sure gutty. I was rooting for you."

"My husband," Nadia said, "is a very brave man."

"And handsome, too, as you told me at your house. And faithful, as you must have ample enough reason to know."

"You bastard," she said.

"Liar, blabbermouth, weasel and now bastard. Nadia, we're not going to make it."

"Yes, we are," she said. "Let's have another bottle of wine."

We had come in her car, a Rolls Corniche. On

the way back, I told her, "Drop me off at the police station. I know some of the boys there. Maybe I can learn why the Feds are in town."

"For us or for CANA?" Stu asked.

"For me," I said. "I'd hate to think Joe Puma was what he's beginning to look like. He left behind a brave wife and a wonderful son."

On this wine-induced sentimental note we parted. I went in to see if Vogel was in his office. He wasn't. I had nowhere to go but home.

And then I realized a mission of mercy was due Calvin. I climbed into the Mustang and drove back to Arroyo Road.

He was pouring gasoline from a can into his tank. He studied me doubtfully. "Now what?"

"I wanted to talk to you without the fuzz listening. Get the new points in? She ready to roll?"

"We'll see."

He went to the front of the car, took the lid off the air cleaner and poured some gas down the carburetor throat.

"Cross your fingers," he said, and climbed in behind the wheel.

The starter groaned twice and died. "Shit!" he said. He looked at me. "That battery's been standing too long. You wouldn't want to run it down to the Mobil station, would you? They got one of those quick chargers there."

"No need," I said. "I've got jumper cables."

I took them out of the trunk and came back to open the hood. I was clipping them to my battery when he said, "Is that a Dalton four-barrel carb?"

"It is. And those are Spelke high-turbulence heads. And Norm Spelke reground my cams."

"Man!" he said. "I knew you were all right the second I saw you."

"You don't have to con me, Calvin. I'm not a cop. I'm a friend of the man who was killed."

He was clipping the other ends of the cables to his battery. "He was a private eye. You a private eye?"

"I was. I'm retired. Okay, let's go."

I started my engine; he tried his starter. Bingo! The dead Plymouth was reborn. I turned off my engine. We disconnected the cables. The Plymouth kept chugging away.

"You want a drink?" he asked.

"I don't think so. I'm overloaded with wine."

"What the hell, man, a little nip won't hurt. We'll drink it out here. The house is kind of in a mess today."

*Today*, that was a clever touch. "Okay," I said.

"All I got is bourbon?"

"What else would I drink?"

"Right. That Vogel, he probably drinks Scotch." He went to the house.

What he had called a nip was a half glass of colorless corn. We went over to sit on the edge of his sagging porch. I sat to the right of him, where he couldn't see me spill some on the ground between sips. It was acid red-eye.

"Got a friend who makes it," he informed me. "What's on your mind?"

"You. You said you once lived in Nevada."

"I did. Drove a cab in Vegas for twelve years."

"And still you go mouthing off in bars about those Nevada men that you saw checking out Puma's car?"

"I was stoned that night. I ain't said nothing since. And I ain't been to Barney's since I started buying this stuff."

"Does Barney know where you live?"

He shook his head. "And I ain't got no phone. So how they going to find me? And why should they? I couldn't identify 'em."

I pointed toward the ocean. "Do you know who lives up there in those beachfront homes?"

"A lot of rich people."

"Including Tony Romolo."

"Last I heard, Romolo lives in Palm Springs in the winter and Cape Cod in the summer. At least his old man did."

"His old man is in a federal penitentiary. Tony moved up here a couple years ago."

"Screw him," Calvin said. "Who cares?"

"I do." I gave him three twenties and my card. "You see any more Nevada cars going along that road, phone me. Anything else you learn, I'd like to know. Okay?"

"You've got a deal. Thanks, buddy."

I didn't head for home. I turned left, toward the ocean. Where Arroyo Road ended at Ocean Drive, I turned right. Maybe Romolo's name would be on his mailbox.

It wasn't. But a few hundred feet from a massive pair of wrought-iron gates that guarded the driveway of a shrub-hidden home, a yellow Pinto was parked. The Yosemite sticker was still on the windshield.

Even the private eyes on the boob tube knew enough to drive inconspicuous cars. If the Feds would get as organized as the hoodlums we could get this country moving again.

I drove to the end of Ocean Drive, turned around in the cul-de-sac, and headed for home. I waved to Mr. X as I drove past.

**11**

THERE WAS THE BUZZ OF CONVERSATION from two tables of bridge in the Callahan wigwam. I nodded and smiled at all the girls (to use a euphemism) and went into the den. Jan had put my Puma papers in there when she cleaned the dining room.

There was no listing for Romolo in the phone book. Information advised me they had no listing for him. One of Joe's unidentified numbers had the first three digits that would encompass that area. I dialed it.

I had guessed right. "The Romolo residence," a haughty British voice answered.

I was about to hang up when this screw must have come loose in my brain. "Is Tony there?" I asked.

"May I have your name, sir?"

"He'll know who I am. I'm calling from Miami. Just give him this message—we don't like what he's doing. You tell him that."

"I don't quite understand, sir."

"You're not supposed to. Just tell him."

"Perhaps it would be better if you—"

"Tell him!" I said, and hung up.

Gas rumbled in my stomach. I went to the kitchen for the Alka Seltzer. Damn you, Joe.... Vogel was right, that lard-ass cop was right. Lowell Kendfelt probably hadn't been lying. Damn you....

Easy now, this would be evidence too circumstantial to convict a man. It's too circumstantial to judge Joe. Get the facts, peeper. No judge or jury would convict a man because he had the private phone number of a hoodlum. Get the facts, peeper.

Brave Brock Callahan, threatening the Mafia from the coward's sanctuary of anonymity. It was almost funny. But who dared to go up against them? They owned politicians and corporations and cops. They ran all the commercial vices in the country that grossed more than two dollars a bet or ten dollars a trick. They had legitimate front organizations in every major capital in the world.

If they had propositioned Joe—what could he say? He could have said no. Why else was he dead?

The gas stopped rumbling in my stomach. The chatter from the living room ceased. Jan came into the den.

"Why are you sitting here glowering?"

"I'm a little bilious. I had lunch with the Engelkes and went overboard on the wine."

"Are they nice?"

"I liked them."

"Then I probably will, too. I polled the girls. They all like Nadia. And the ones who have met her husband like him. Lois said Nadia has the money and tries to dominate the mouse."

"*Lois* said that?"

"I know, I know. The pot was talking about the kettle."

"Let me tell you two things. The man is no mouse. And no human or animal, female or male, is going to dominate him."

"Okay. I've been wrong before. Should we eat out?"

"Any place but Pierre's. Some place that serves bland food."

"I'll call Nadia first," she said. "I thought we could have a barbecue Friday night."

At Castellini's Lobster House, Jan had lobster. I had clam chowder and rye rolls. The Castellini family were third generation San Valdesto residents. They were fishermen, poor at first, now rich.

The old-country Italians had come here to fish or farm. They raised grapes, oranges, lemons, avocados or walnuts. They made wine. They worked hard and prospered.

The Italian-Americans we were getting now had made their fortunes in other towns in less-honorable endeavors.

I told Jan about the fireworks in Stuart Engelke's office.

"She sounds like a tigress," Jan said. "Lois told me her father was Russian and her mother was Spanish."

"Was? Are they dead?"

"They died two years ago, Lois said. Their car

went out of control and over a cliff at Big Sur. That's when Nadia inherited all of her money."

"Lois should work for the F.B.I."

"You don't like her much, do you?"

"I love her! But she's so damned—stuffy."

"Not as stuffy as Alan."

"That's true. Let me rephrase it. She's so damned—social?"

Jan shook her head. "You missed it again. What she is, is dumb. But, like you, all her instincts are sound."

Instinct wasn't enough, not in this mess. It had served me often, my hunter's instinct. In this one, if you don't mind a mixed metaphor, I had a feeling I was swimming in water too deep for me.

"Why don't we go to a movie?" Jan asked. "We haven't been to a movie for ages."

I forget the name of the movie but Burt Reynolds was in it. He is no Olivier, I grant you, but I love to watch him work, so free and easy.

Every time there was a fade-out, I waited for the commercial. I had forgotten that movies don't have commercials. They have to be the best bargain in our inflated economy; for only a few extra dollars you can avoid deodorant and toilet-paper ads.

In my feature dream of the night, Nadia explained to me that the Feds were in town because her father was a Russian spy. I assured her in my smooth Burt Reynolds way that there was no need to worry; I could handle the Feds.

Jan was preparing breakfast in the morning

when I asked, "Why don't we invite the Vogels to the barbecue? We owe them."

"Wouldn't those people bore Bernie? He's kind of bright."

"And I'm not?"

"Do you want rolls or toast?"

"Answer me."

"Another thing," she said, "Bernie doesn't know about the Engelkes, does he? What if Nadia or her husband should mention to him that she hired Joe?"

"That's the last thing they're likely to mention. Wait—how do you know I kept that from Bernie?"

"Because I know you."

"You're so perceptive! I'm surprised that you married such a dumb lout."

"It was sheer animal attraction. Toast or rolls?"

"Rolls."

"I'll invite the Vogels," she said.

When I got to the station, the desk sergeant informed me that Vogel was in Chief Harris's office. I sat and sat and finally said, "Tell Vogel I'll be back later—maybe."

"Maybe?"

"That's right—*maybe*!"

He sighed. "Poor Bernie! I'm sure he'll miss seeing you. I'll tell him."

I wasn't getting the proper respect at home or in the field this morning. I turned my broad back on the smart-ass and went out to my car. I headed for the Puma residence.

Ellen Puma was out in front trying to cut the gray Bermuda grass on the front lawn with a rusty twelve-inch hand mower.

"Here," I said. "I'll do that. Joey should do it."

"He's in Fullerton at a track meet. I can handle it."

"You go sit in the shade," I said.

It was a small lawn but a dull mower. Twenty minutes later, hot and sweaty, I had gnawed away enough of the grass with those rusty blades to make it almost respectable.

"A Coke?" Ellen asked. "A beer? Seven-Up?"

"Seven-Up would suit me fine."

"We'll drink it in the backyard," she said. "The neighbors have enough to gossip about already."

On the back steps, looking out at all her flowers, she asked, "Have you learned why tne F.B.I. is so interested?"

"No. It's probably that Scarlatti business."

"Every Christmas for the last three," she said, "he's sent us a check for five hundred dollars."

"Vince Scarlatti?"

"No, no. The boy, Peter. He's grown up now."

"He must be nicer than Vince. How about you? Find a job?"

"I have my application in at seven law offices in town. Nothing yet."

"I'll be talking with Judge Vaughan Friday night. He might know some lawyer who can use a trained secretary."

"I'd appreciate that." She smiled. "If he knows of more than one, I'll take the single one."

"Lawyers get rich so quickly he'd have to be young to stay unmarried."

She shrugged. "We can hope."

"You're back with the living, aren't you? You are one gutty kid, Ellen Puma."

"And you are one great guy," she said. "Happily married I suppose?"

"Very happily."

"That's the way my luck has been running lately. Damn that Joe! What was he doing in that godforsaken place?"

"I intend to find out. Hang in there, Ellen."

"You, too," she said. "And bless you."

Vogel was still at the station when I got back. But he was talking in the hallway with Mr. X. I ducked into the men's room to stay out of sight.

He opened the door a few minutes later and smiled at me. "You can come out now. That guy must have given you a real whomping."

"He's lucky to be alive. What's on the agenda for today?"

"I thought we'd go out and talk with Tony Romolo."

And the butler could recognize my voice. I said, "I'll wait in the car. You're official; I'm not. I don't want that Mafia on my neck."

"I won't introduce you. And if you can keep your big mouth shut, they won't have any reason to bump you."

"I won't say a word," I promised.

In the department's car, he said, "Hiding in toilets and waiting in cars. When did you turn gutless?"

Nothing from me.

"I was joking," he said. "You'll never run out of mouth or guts."

"When I do, I'll go back to golf. You're coming to our house Friday night. We're having a barbecue."

"It's news to me."

"Elly will inform you when you get home."

"I usually play poker on Friday nights."

"You fight that out with Elly."

"Oh, sure! We'll be at your house. Should I wear a tie?"

"For a barbecue? Why don't you wear that dumb leisure suit of yours?"

"Now we're even," he said.

Never get mad, get even, John F. Kennedy had said. Get even with the Mafia? Dear departed president, it's like this, you see....

There was no Plymouth parked next to Calvin's mansion. I hoped he wasn't at Barney's.

There was a telephone in one of the huge stone pillars that held up the wrought-iron gates. Vogel got out to identify himself and came back to the car. The big gates swung open and we drove through.

"The slimy scum sure live high on the hog, don't they?" he asked.

He wasn't expecting an answer and I was practicing silence. I said nothing. There was a Porsche in sight on the long curving driveway, an Aston-Martin and a BMW. There was no big black car with Nevada plates.

The butler said, "This way, Lieutenant," and led us into an immense two-story gabled living room at the back of the house. Wide windows gave us an impressive view of the sea.

Tony Romolo stood in the center of the room, tall, slim, dark and handsome. He was wearing white tennis shorts and a yellow cashmere pullover sweater.

"Well, gentlemen, what can I do for you?"

"We're investigating the death of a man named Joseph Puma," Vogel said.

Romolo nodded. "I read about that."

"The night he was killed," Vogel said, "one of our officers saw a big black car come out from the parking lot where Puma was found dead and head this way."

Romolo frowned. "I'm not sure just what you're suggesting, Lieutenant, but I have a feeling my attorney should be present."

"That's up to you. We can wait."

He looked between us doubtfully. Then he said, "Go on."

"The officer had no reason to suspect anything at the time, so he didn't get the license number of the car. But he remembered they were Nevada plates."

"So?"

"I would have to assume you have friends in Nevada, Mr. Romolo."

"Why would you have to assume that?"

Vogel's voice was harsher. "Let's not play games."

Tony Romolo took a deep breath and exhaled it. "Lieutenant, I may have investments in Nevada, but I can't think of any close friends I have there. I have investments in a number of states, including this one."

"That would include the Trinity Investment Company?"

"It might. I would have to ask my business manager. Should I phone him?"

"Don't bother," Vogel said. "He's probably as crooked as you are."

"I think," Romolo said, "it is time for you gentlemen to leave."

"So do I," Vogel said. "I've got a weak stomach."

We went out through the door the butler opened for us. We went back to the department car parked among all that classy machinery and climbed in. The gates swung open for us.

Vogel's face was stone. I waited for a mile or so until it was hard clay before asking, "Who told you about Tony's investment in Trinity?"

"That would be police business."

"Pardon me for asking. Mr. X probably told you. Are you two buddy-buddy now?"

"Shut up!"

"Screw you," I said. "Put on your leisure suit and go play poker Friday night."

About a tenth of a mile later he started to laugh. "That really is a dumb suit, isn't it?"

"I'm surprised Elly let you buy it. I admired the way you covered for Calvin. I didn't think you liked him."

"I love that ornery bastard. But he's on the wrong side of the fence."

The law, that was the fence to Bernie. Not justice, but the law. I considered explaining to him that everything Hitler did was legal, but it didn't seem like the right time to mention it.

Vincent Scarlatti was an old man. Had he turned over the reins to Peter, as Nick Romolo had to his son? In that case, the five-hundred-dollar Christmas check could be a retainer. The sons may not have inherited their fathers' enmities. Once again, Joe could have been the liaison man for the Scarlattis, patching up a family feud.

"Why so silent?" Vogel asked.

"I've been thinking about the Scarlattis and the Romolos. Are they still feuding?"

"I don't know. Why?"

"For the last three years Joe Puma has been getting a five-hundred-dollar Christmas check from Peter Scarlatti."

"Where'd you learn that?"

"From my new buddy, Mr. X."

He said wearily, "Let's stop taking cheap shots at each other. Let's pretend we're adults."

"Mrs. Puma told me this morning."

"Did she tell you anything else?"

"Only that she's looking for a job and her son was at a track meet. I was thinking the five hundred could be a retainer. I had this crazy theory."

"I'll listen."

"Joe could have been the peacemaker. Peter could have used him to approach the Romolos and patch things up. Tony doesn't need any gang wars. They don't work that crudely these days."

"Sometimes they do. But you can imagine an old pro like Puma meeting hoodlums at night in a deserted place like that?"

"If Romolo thought his house was being watched, why not? Joe wasn't bringing trouble. He was bringing a peace offer. All they had to do was say no."

He shook his head. "I don't buy it."

Joe the peacemaker? Blessed are the peacemakers; for they shall be called the children of God. . . . I couldn't quite sell it to myself.

"Maybe," Vogel said. "Maybe. And their answer was a bullet in the eye. But what hit man could carry a puny little thirty-two?"

"In the eye, a pellet gun would do the trick. He must have trusted the killer, to let him get that close."

"I suppose," he said in a tired voice. "I blew my cool back there, didn't I? That smooth bastard really got to me. With their lawyers and their slick accountants and their phony fronts. They make a mockery of the law."

"It's our law, not theirs. They found all the holes in it. And their high-priced shysters taught them how to bend it."

"Maybe we should, too."

"Not you, Bernie. Then you'd be just another crummy private eye. I like you the way you are."

His smile was dim. "You're kind of moral, Brock. Even if you did quit going to Mass."

"So are you. Even though you don't go to temple anymore."

"You slob," he said. "I'll buy you lunch."

At Plotkin's Kitchen he had lox, I had corned beef. He had four cigarettes and three cups of coffee. I had two cups of coffee.

"You should quit smoking," I said.

"I know, I know. I've tried a dozen times. I should quit the department, too. But I can't afford to. You know what a cop is today? He's nothing! The citizens scorn him. The shysters make a damned fool out of him in court. He picks up some punk on a lousy traffic violation and winds up with a bullet in his head. And who cares?"

"Some of us do."

"Not enough of you."

"Enough. You get too bitter about it and we'll wind up with a police state. I'm sure neither one of us wants that, do we?"

"I'm beginning to think it's the only answer."

"So did Stalin and Hitler. Where do we go next?"

"I haven't any place. You?"

I shook my head.

"Okay. You go out and play golf and I'll go back to the station to see if your beloved Mr. X has come up with something. If he has, I'll have you paged at the country club."

"You said no more cheap shots," I reminded him.

"I apologize. Let's go."

## 12

HE WENT INTO THE STATION. I went home. Jan was out at poolside reading a big, fat novel under the shade of the overhang.

"Some man phoned," she told me. "He wants you to phone him back. I left the number on the desk in the den."

"Didn't he leave his name?"

"Only the number."

It looked dimly familiar. I checked it; it was one of the numbers on Joe's list of four. The initials were S.H.

The voice that answered the phone was old but hearty. "Brock Callahan returning your call," I said.

"Oh, yes," he said. "Judge Vaughan told me yesterday that you were a friend of Joseph Puma's."

"I was."

"And you're a private detective?"

"Not anymore. I'm retired."

"Could you come up here to Ridge Road this afternoon? I know it's a long drive but I'm confined to a wheelchair and it's my driver's day off. I would be glad to compensate you for your time, of course."

"No need for that. I'll be there."

He gave me his name, Sloan Hartford, and the address. Ridge Road ran along the peak high above our house, but the address he gave me was at the other end of it.

I took the freeway to the Jacinto turnoff and started to climb. Up, up, up, winding and twisting, the view getting wider, the Mustang complaining. She hates to work. Zipping along the freeways, that is her idea of the good life.

His house was on the west side of the road, a low, long redwood place cantilevered out over nothing but air. The way I saw it, a six-point earthquake could slide him right back to town—in many pieces. He must be a brave old man.

A heavy black woman of about fifty opened the door to my ring. She led me to a corner room with about twelve feet of air below it.

He was old, he was thin. But his color was good and his handshake was strong. "Alan isn't usually wrong about people. He was sure you'd come up here."

I said nothing.

He pointed at a rattan armchair. "Sit down, Mr. Callahan."

"I realize bringing you up here was an imposition," he said. "But since a horse threw me, thirty years ago, I've been shackled to this thing."

"Wouldn't living in town be more convenient for you?"

"It would. But I grew up in this house. I've learned to rely on others, of course. One man I relied on was Judson Barlow. He convinced me, some months ago, to invest a sizable portion of my capital in the Trinity Investment Company. Do you know anything about it?''

"Very little. Mostly rumors.''

"I suppose the rumors would be about criminal involvement?''

I nodded.

"I asked my friend Chief Harris about those rumors. He knew nothing. I then tried to hire your friend Mr. Puma to investigate the rumors for me. He refused the job. He said it would be a conflict of interest.''

"In what way? How?''

"He told me he was already employed by the Trinity Investment Company.''

"When was this?''

"Three days before he was found dead.''

"Have you talked about this with Judson Barlow?''

He shook his head. "I've steered clear of him ever since the rumors. Would you be interested in doing the investigation for me, Mr. Callahan?''

"I'm retired.''

"I'd make it worth your while.''

"I don't work for pay anymore. But I am working with Lieutenant Vogel on Joe's murder. I'll tell him what you told me.'' I paused. "Besides the rumors I've heard, I learned something more solid this morning. I'm almost sure the justice department is investigating the Trinity Investment Company. If it's possible for you to get out now without losing much, it might be wise.''

"You don't think it will be a profitable investment?"

"It could be. But whether the profits will ever filter down to all the investors could be doubtful."

"I understand. Skimming. A touch of corn, Mr. Callahan?"

"I don't know. I've still got to get down that road."

"Wild Turkey."

"I'm sold."

"Would you tell my housekeeper? She's probably in the kitchen. I'll have mine straight."

I went to the kitchen and relayed his request and came back to sit down again. "Have you known Judson Barlow long?"

"Since he was a kid. He worked on one of my ranches in the summer. A wild kid from a good family, but I always liked him."

The housekeeper came in with our drinks. "You know, Mr. Hartford, that this is strictly against the doctor's orders."

"Doctors don't give me orders, Lydia. And this is my first today."

"And your last!" she said. She went back to the kitchen.

He shook his head and sighed. "She's so bossy. If she wasn't the best cook in the country, I wouldn't take it. I may fire her one of these days."

"How long has she been with you?"

"Thirty years."

I laughed, and so did he. "She's a goddamned

saint, that's what she is. Sticking with a sour apple like me."

I said, "For some reason Joe Puma kept your telephone number in a private file of his. Since he had already rejected your offer, I wonder why he'd keep the number?"

"It's an unlisted number. Perhaps he kept it in the event he changed his mind. Perhaps Trinity wasn't willing to pay him as much as I might. Investigation is a business, too, isn't it? I mean, you boys aren't in it for your health."

"No. Nor money alone, either. I don't know."

He smiled. "Yes, you do. I've shot big game all over the world. It's the hunt, isn't it?"

"Probably."

He shook his head again. "Judson was always blustery and inclined to bullshit people. But I can't see him tied up with real criminals."

"He might not know they are."

"That could be. He was never very bright. I doubt if he'd have his job at the university if his father hadn't donated that field house. And being a friend of the governor's helped, I'm sure."

"Probably. Vogel and I will talk with him. We won't mention your name."

He smiled. "I understand from Chief Harris that Vogel is a whiz at poker. Maybe we could arrange a game some night?"

"Bernie's a friend of mine," I said, "but I don't play high-stakes poker with him. I'm not that rich."

"Just a thought I had," he said. "I've had to get my excitement sitting down for the last thirty years." He raised his glass. "Here's to us, Mr. Callahan, and to hell with the rest of 'em."

We drank to that and I headed down the mountain.

A horseman, a rancher, a poker player, a big-game hunter and Wild Turkey drinker living on that precarious perch in a chair for thirty years. Maybe Bernie and I owed him a high-stakes game. Maybe, between us, we could stick it to good old Bernie.

I phoned good old Bernie at six o'clock at home. I told him what Sloan Hartford had told me.

He said, "We'll go out to the university and talk with Barlow tomorrow. I'll set it up."

"Hartford suggested that we get together for some poker. I guess he wants to test himself. He's heard of your great skill at the game."

"And I've heard of his. No, thanks. I'll see you in the morning."

The man who had insulted Tony Romolo that morning was afraid to go up against an old man in a wheelchair. Nobody is brave all the time.

Over my bottle of Einlicher and her martini, Jan asked, "What did that man want with you? Who was he?"

"His name is Sloan Hartford and he is an investor in the Trinity Investment Company."

"And?"

"And he's worried. For reasons we've discussed before."

"And what was that about the poker?"

"Hartford wanted to go up against Bernie. Bernie declined."

"I hope you weren't planning to get into the game. Bernie told me you're the worst poker player in the world."

I made no comment.

"Could we play gin rummy after dinner?" she asked. "There's nothing decent on TV."

She took eighteen dollars and forty-two cents away from me before we quit to watch the eleven o'clock news.

There had been another radiation leak at a nuclear power plant in Pennsylvania. Families in the area were forced to find temporary shelter out of the danger zone.

Jan kept muttering as she watched. "The bastards!" she said.

Five congressmen and one senator had been trapped by an undercover operation of the F.B.I. They had been indicted for taking bribes from agents disguised as representing Arab oil interests.

"The bastards!" I said. "All Democrats."

Nothing from her but a glare.

Two Los Angeles police officers had pumped nine bullets into an unarmed one-hundred-and-thirty pound black man in the central district of the town. The officers claimed the man had attacked them.

That was enough bastards for one night. We turned off the tube and went to bed.

Shadows on the moonlit windows and rustlings in the shrubs. A siren wailed from the direction of the freeway. The dog across the street began to bark. I finally fell asleep around one o'clock.

At ten o'clock the next morning Vogel and I were in the office of Judson Barlow out at the U.S.C.V. campus.

The bull sat in his big chair behind his big desk and told us, "I hired Puma, not the company. I control fifty-three percent of the stock in the Trinity Investment Company. Who told you I hired Puma?"

"His file cabinet," Vogel lied. "Could I ask why you felt you needed his services?"

"Both of you live in this town. You must know about the crazy rumors that have been circulating. I heard yesterday that even some F.B.I. men are interested."

"They haven't contacted you?"

"Not yet."

"So you hired Mr. Puma to learn if the rumors were true?"

"Of course not! I hired him to find out who was spreading them. Wouldn't I know if they were true?"

"Isn't Tony Romolo one of your investors?"

"I never heard of him."

"How about the Mead Land Company?"

"They've invested some money. Quite a lot, as a matter of fact."

"Tony Romolo *is* the Mead Land Company, Professor. And there's a possibility he is the man who had Joe Puma killed."

The bull seemed to shrink behind his desk. If you gave him an enema, Lenny had said, you could bury him in a match box.

He looked between us dazedly. Stupidly might

be a better choice of words. "You mean this Romolo is a—a—".

"We're not sure what he is," Vogel said. "His father is in a federal penitentiary for running the same operations Tony is now running. I'm surprised that you haven't heard of that name."

"I, uh, don't read much outside of the geology journals. I'm sure my attorney will find a way to get me out of this—this mess."

"Advise him not to move too fast," Vogel said. "That could have been Puma's mistake."

The bull nodded weakly. He was ready for the matador's blade.

"Is there any information you can give us," Vogel asked, "that might possibly help us find Puma's murderer?"

"None. Maybe my attorney could. His name is Knox Hamilton. Do you know him?"

Vogel nodded. "Thank you for seeing us, Professor." Outside the sun was shining. Some students were hurrying, some were strolling between the buildings. There was a smell of the ocean in the light breeze.

"Knox Hamilton next?" I asked.

"I don't think so. He has a law degree but most of his work is investment advice. He's managed to put a couple of Montevista widows on welfare with his advice. If his old man hadn't been rich Knox would have wound up drinking muscatel in a doorway on lower Main Street."

"You sound bitter, Bernie."

"I keep running into millionaire nitwits and wonder why I'm so poor."

"Elly told me you could have retired comfortably two years ago. She said you'll never retire."

"What does she know?"

"One thing she knows for sure is poor mouth Bernard Vogel. If not Hamilton, where?"

"Nowhere," he said. "Let the damned Feds handle it. Let them earn their ridiculous salaries. I've got a desk piled high with overdue reports right now. Maybe tomorrow. I'll call you."

"Where is Hamilton's office?"

"In the Barlow Building. Where else?"

Bernie knew how to milk a four-card flush but the stock market had burned him. We rode down to the station without further dialogue.

In the parking lot, I said, "If Hamilton knows anything that might be useful, I'll bring it to you. Otherwise—tomorrow?"

"If we have some place to go. Don't slug any more G-men. They might be our last best hope."

"I won't. Cheer up, Bernie!"

"I'll whistle while I type," he said.

Driving around, asking questions, what a tiring and frustrating way to spend a day or earn a living. Census takers know that. That's why they work only one year out of ten.

The slim, tall secretary in Hamilton's office asked me the question they are all taught the first day in secretarial school. "Do you have an appointment?"

*No* was the proper answer. This time I said, "Do I need one?"

Her smile was charming. "Not with me you

don't. But Mr. Hamilton is more formal. Why don't you tell me who you are and why you're here?''

"My name is Brock Callahan. I'm here because Judson Barlow suggested I see your boss. How's that?''

"That gets you in there," she said. She pressed a button and announced me on her intercom.

I should have stayed in the outer office. The scenery had been better. Hamilton obviously knew nothing about the Mead Land Company and so he tried to avoid revealing his ignorance by double-talking in legalese. He was familiar with the name of Tony Romolo; he thought Tony was an operatic tenor. It couldn't have been easy, but the bull had found a man in town who knew less than he did.

I thanked him in the middle of one of his longer sentences and left.

I had a new motive for the murder of Joe Puma. Barlow had hired him to smoke out Romolo and Tony had learned about it.

But why then were there no investigative reports in Joe's private file? If they had been in his office file, both the police and the government men would have interviewed Barlow by now. Had the bull lied?

Joe wouldn't have been likely to try to blackmail Romolo for thirty thousand dollars or even thirty cents. Hoodlums spend their money on politicians and expensive attorneys. A lousy private eye who threatened them would wind up crippled or dead, and Joe knew it.

Somewhere in this muddled case there was an angle that I was overlooking.

Vogel was depending on the Feds. In the last two days he had spent only the mornings on the murder of a San Valdesto citizen. Even a liquor-store holdup got more police time than that.

I went home. Jan wasn't there. I worked with the weights for about fifteen minutes and then swam twenty leisurely lengths of the pool. After my shower I went back to Joe's notes.

There was one number left of the four identified by initials. I dialed it. The mechanical voice of a recorder suggested I consult my phone book. I had dialed a number that didn't exist.

I was recradling the phone when the doorbell rang.

It was Calvin. "I'm scared," he said.

**13**

"COME IN," I SAID. "What happened?"

He came in and I closed the door.

"A couple guys were in Barney's, asking about me. Thank God Barney doesn't know where I live. There was a friend of mine in there. He came out to the house to tell me."

"Maybe they were federal officers."

"I doubt it like hell. My friends said they were driving a black Chrysler Cordoba with Nevada plates. Man, that has to be the same car I saw that night!"

"I think we'd better go downtown and tell the police about this."

"Like hell. I'm getting out of town. I thought, maybe, if you could lend me some money—I'll pay it back."

"That would be a stupid move. The police might want to question you again, and the federal men might, too. And you can't hide from the hoodlums, not on this planet."

"So what do I do—hang myself?"

The image of the crippled eagle up there on his Ridge Road perch came to me. Crazy, maybe, but. . . .

"Sit down, Calvin," I told him. "I have to make a call." I went into the den and phoned Sloan Hartford.

I explained the situation to him, and asked, "Do you have a guest house or something up there? I didn't notice any."

"No. But there's plenty of room in the house. And I could use some company. Send him up."

"He's not always, well, clean—and—"

"Brock, I have shared quarters with cannibals, pygmies, and second lieutenants. I'm sure he will be better company than that. And Lydia will see that he stays reasonably clean."

"It could be dangerous."

"That's the part that decided me," he said. "Quit stalling!"

I told Calvin where the house was and asked him, "Do you still have some of that money I gave you?"

"I ran it up to two hundred," he told me. "It ain't likely I'll need more than that if I stay in town and have free board."

"You gamble?"

"I play a little cards now and then."

"Calvin, I think you'll find a home up there on Ridge Road. I'll stay in touch. Vogel and I will be looking for those men."

"Okay. But if I get cabin fever up there, I'm taking off."

"If you play cards with your host, you'll be taking off broke. And soon dead. Those creeps have stoolies all over the country. Wise up!"

"I'll be careful," he promised.

Oh sure. Where had he ever learned to be careful? You don't wind up in a shack on Arroyo Road by being careful. You wind up in Montevista, rich and dull.

Jan came home about an hour after he left. "Lois," she told me, "had Nadia as a fill-in again today. She is nice, isn't she? Opinionated, though."

"I know."

"And a wild bidder," my bride added. "She cost me a dollar and eighty-five cents when she was my partner."

"She goes for broke?"

"Does she ever! And how was your day?"

"Short and depressing. We had nowhere to go this afternoon."

"You're depressed and I'm bored. How would you feel about it if I went back to work?"

Jan had been an interior decorator before we were married. I said, "Anything that makes you happy. Do you mean running your own shop or working for somebody else?"

"For Kay Decor. Audrey Kay suggested it the other day. And Lois has finally found me a good housekeeper."

"It should be more interesting than bridge and chitchat."

"God, yes! And booze. The way some of those women drink! I can understand now why you go plodding around with Bernie."

"I think Bernie's stopped plodding on the Puma murder."

"But not you, I'll bet. You're no quitter."

"Not yet."

"My bulldog!" she said. "Give me a big kiss and a hug."

I was getting a little old for some homilies. It's always darkest right before dawn was one of them. I had grown up on homilies in Long Beach, discarded some and stuck with others. There was no dawn in sight on this one and might never be.

Joe was dead; nobody could bring him back. Because Joe was dead, Calvin had to hide. Who would be next? The mob could keep the dawn away forever.

I called Bernie at dinnertime and told him about Calvin's visit and the two men in the black Chrysler.

"I'll send out a call for them. We can bring them in for questioning, if nothing else. Did Calvin go back to his house?"

"No. He wanted to leave town. I stashed him away up in Sloan Hartford's mountain retreat. You don't want to go with me and look up those two men?"

"Why? The uniformed boys will be looking for them."

"I thought maybe you could show your badge to make it legal, and then I could muscle 'em."

"You're mental," he said. "You've been watching too much TV. You got a death wish or something?"

"Nope. Only the normal quota of citizen indignation. Should I come in tomorrow, sir?"

"Not in the morning. I'm about a third of the

way through those reports that were due day before yesterday."

"Okay!" I hung up.

I cooled off a little during the night and decided to go down in the morning. The private file had been deciphered to my present ability; maybe Bernie would let me examine what they had from Joe's office file.

Bernie's office was blue with cigarette smoke. He looked up from behind his desk and grinned at me. "Still miffed?"

"No. I wondered if I could look at Joe's office files."

"If you want. There are forty-three cases in there and every one of the people involved has been interrogated. Maybe it would better if you just read those reports. Save you a lot of gasoline."

"When did all this happen?"

"Every time an officer had a free hour or two. While you and I were riding around sniping at each other, they were working. You never thought of that, did you?"

I felt about four feet tall. And dumber than the bull.

"Well?" he said.

"I apologize."

"Apology accepted. Anything else?"

"I had this thought. If the men in the black car who were looking for Calvin are the same ones he saw in that parking lot, they couldn't be working for Romolo."

"Why not?"

"Because you had alerted Romolo. He would have sent them home."

"Not if they had alibis. They were picked up last night. They have five people who will testify under oath that they were in El Cajon the night Puma was killed."

I nodded meekly. "I guess I'll go out and play some golf. Sorry to have been such a bother."

"Oy!" he said. "Two hundred and eighteen pounds of petulance. You've been a big help, pal. If anything new develops, you'll be the first I call."

"Thanks. See you tonight."

I didn't feel that golf was my answer. I drove out to Arroyo Road. Maybe I could meet the gray cat again. Maybe he—or she—knew something.

As I drove close to the lot I saw this black car parked in Calvin's driveway. I drove on. I intended to drive past to check the plates, the sane thing to do. But my memory of Sloan Hartford was still strong. I pulled in behind the black Cordoba with the Nevada license.

I was getting out of the car when two men came out of the house. They stopped on the porch to look down at me. They were not wide and swarthy and dressed in dark suits. They were average-size nondescript-type guys. They could have been insurance salesmen or stockbrokers. Both of them wore sports jackets and slacks and loafers.

"Is Calvin home?" I asked them.

"Calvin Ellers?" the one on the right asked. "Is he a friend of yours?"

"Far from it," I said. "Thirteen hundred dollars from it. Are you guys collectors, too?"

The one on the left nodded.

"He's probably on his way to Miami by now," I said. "Well, he paid us off last time he came back from there. He probably will this time."

They looked at each other and again at me. "Miami? What's in Miami? Relatives?"

"His sister lives down there, I guess she married some big shot. That's what Calvin claims, anyway."

"Would you know the name of this big shot? Did Calvin name him?"

"Calvin? You're lucky to get the time of day out of him. He tried to scare me last time. He tried to sell me the story his brother-in-law was a *big* man in the syndicate."

They looked at each other again.

The one on the right asked, "If it's not too personal, would you mind telling me why any store in town would give Ellers thirteen hundred dollars' worth of credit?"

"It isn't a store," I said. "It's a table. Calvin has this habit of drawing to inside straights. You guys from Vegas?"

They shook their heads.

"If you find him in town, would you give me a ring? The boss would appreciate it. It's an unlisted number."

The one on the right took out a ball-point pen and a card. "Shoot," he said.

I gave him the phone number of the police department.

"And if you get anything," the one on the left said, "you could phone us. We're at the Biltmore. Just ask for suite five-twenty-two."

"I'll do that. Good hunting, boys."

It may not have been an Academy-Award performance, but I thought I had brought it off rather well. Even Burt Reynolds would have to admit I played the role with professional insouciance.

In my rearview mirror I could see the Cordoba pull out of Calvin's driveway and once again head toward the ocean. On the road in front of me, coming my way, was a yellow Pinto. Mr. X had scraped the Yosemite sticker off his windshield. In bureaucratic reasoning, that probably made his car inconspicuous. I tooted my horn at him as we passed.

There was the unmistakable smell of Irish stew in the house when I opened the front door. A tall and buxom middle-aged woman in a light blue cotton housedress was in the dining room polishing the silverware.

"Mr. Callahan?" she asked me.

I nodded.

"I'm your new housekeeper. My name is Mary Casey. Your wife is at the market buying some things for tonight. She told me you'd probably be home for lunch."

"And you made us an Irish stew," I said.

"It was your wife's idea. She told me hers have never been exactly to your taste."

This one was. I was back in Long Beach at my mother's table. Conning those hoodlums had diminished some of the humiliation I had suffered in Vogel's office. Mary Casey's Irish stew restored the confidence of my youth. Nobody was going to hold back the dawn forever, not from me.

"Pay her whatever she asks," I told Jan. "Don't let her go."

"Yes, master. But don't expect stew three times a day."

Whole again, and fortified, I went to the den. I wrote down everything I had learned since Joe died and tried to find a pattern in it.

It was still a maze, every passage coming to a dead end.

I phoned Sloan Hartford and asked him, "How are things going?"

"Very well. Lydia goes around sniffing and muttering, but I'm sure she'll adjust to the situation."

"And Calvin?"

"He's interesting company—if a little stubborn. He's into me for fourteen dollars already but he refuses to play for high stakes."

"He's never had much experience at it. Once he builds up his bankroll he might change his attitude."

"Let's hope so. In the meantime he's a lot more fun than the boob tube."

"Let me know if he gets restless. I don't want him out in the open where he's an easy target."

"Neither do I. I sold my Trinity stock. At a profit." He chuckled. "I sold it to Knox Hamilton."

"That wasn't very sporting—shooting fish in a barrel."

"He sold it to me originally. From Judson's holdings. I figured I owed him one. I'll keep in touch."

I went back to the den, back to the maze. I was still looking for a pattern when Jan came in to warn me our guests would soon be arriving.

14

MARY CASEY'S CULINARY MAGIC was not confined to Irish stew. Her hors d'oeuvres were worthy of a French chef. I gladly relinquished my barbecue specialty—burning steaks over charcoal—to her.

After the obligatory opening chat, the company divided as it always does into special-interest groups. Jan, Bernie and Ellen talked about books, Nadia and Lois about the difficulty of finding good domestic help. Alan, Stu and I talked football, the great names, the great games. Nobody mentioned CANA.

A few minutes before we ate I was sitting on the couch with Nadia when she asked quietly, "Did Mr. Puma continue to investigate my husband after I—well, you know—"

"There's no record of it in his files. Why?"

"One of Stu's attorney friends made a remark the other day that made me wonder." She paused. "This is just between us, but Stu was very active in an antinuclear group when we lived in Los Angeles."

"He wasn't working for the company then?"

"No. That was several years ago. It wasn't

South Coast that lured us up here. It was this lovely town.''

"And now I'll share a secret with you," I said. "Puma did some work for the Trinity Investment Company. He was probably working for them when he died.''

"Working to discredit Stu?''

I shrugged.

She put her hand on mine. "This was your idea, wasn't it, having us at your party?''

"Not completely.''

She patted my hand. "You are a good man, Callahan.''

"Careful!'' I said. "Stu is looking our way. You know how jealous he can be.''

"You are a good man,'' she repeated. "With a nasty tongue.''

It was Judge Vaughan who suggested a little poker after we had eaten. I saw Bernie's eyes light up.

Then Jan added, "Nickel limit, though. And only one raise a round.'' The light in Bernie's eyes went out.

Lois was the big winner. She bet every hand and then laid out her cards at the end so we could tell her if she had won or lost. Because the predominant choice of most dealers was seven-card stud, there would not be enough cards for all if everybody stayed. So we added four aces from another deck. Seven-card stud with eight aces and the black cards wild can eliminate the skill element in the game. I was the second-biggest winner.

Judge Vaughan had given me the name of a young attorney who had told him this morning that he was looking for a secretary he could afford. Ellen Puma had once told me she was an addict of the late movies on TV. When our guests left before midnight, I phoned her.

"His name is Park Livett," I said. "I called tonight so that you can get him at home before he leaves for the office. That should be an edge. Judge Vaughan said you could mention his name. That could be another edge."

"You are a saint," she said. "A damned saint!"

I had started the day as a lamebrain in Bernie's office and ended it as a saint. Not a bad day, all in all.

Mrs. Casey had gone to bed. Jan was emptying ashtrays and stacking glasses in the dishwasher. "It went off well, didn't it?" she said.

"I thought so."

"I was wrong about Stu Engelke. He's no mouse."

Nothing from me.

"And Monday I go back to work," she said. "I never thought I'd look forward to going back to work. When it's work you enjoy, it's different, isn't it?"

"And the most fun," I added, "when you don't have to do it for a living."

"That's another thing I thought would never happen."

"What?"

"Agreeing with you," she said.

It was drizzling outside when we went to bed.

It was pouring in the morning when we got up. Rain in May is rare in our town. It came down in sheets all morning, setting a new weather-bureau record for the month.

Last winter's fire had destroyed the watershed on the hills above our house. I was out with the neighbors before lunch, digging trenches and filling sandbags as the mud started sliding down the hills toward us.

Jan was out there, too. Most of the wives were working with us and most of the kids. We were back to the pioneer days, working shoulder to shoulder to save our homes.

The rain began to taper off, but the mud kept coming down the road, spilling over the curbs and onto the lawns, oozing toward our front doors.

It was touch and go—and a bad time for Mr. X to come splashing through the puddles toward me.

"I have to talk with you," he said.

"Later!"

"Now," he said.

I took a step toward him, my trenching spade raised. "Mister," I said, "grab a shovel and start filling sandbags or get the hell out of here!"

He stared at me and then at the spade.

From behind him, our appointed neighborhood leader, Art Lucie, said, "Here you are, skinny. You can spell me. I'm going for coffee."

Mr. X took the shovel and started to fill sandbags.

Around two o'clock, Jan said, "I think we've

got it under control. I'll go to the house and tell
Mrs. Casey. Will there be three for lunch?"

"Hungry, Mr. X?" I asked.

"My name is David Delamater," he said, "and
I'm hungry."

"Okay, Dave. We'll have a drink first."

"You're beginning to sound human," he said.

He hung his wet clothes in the laundry room. I
gave him a shirt and a pair of jeans to put on. In
the den, I asked, "Scotch, bourbon, vodka, gin,
wine—what's your pleasure?"

"Bourbon and ice. Not too much ice."

I made it and handed it to him. "Where's that
little yellow Pinto? I didn't see it out there."

"I rented a more inconspicuous car," he explained. "I—we are going into a different phase
of this case. I used the Pinto when I wanted to be
seen. You could call that the intimidation phase.
Now, we're in the investigative phase."

"That probably makes sense," I said. "But not
to me."

"I can't tell you any more. Do you have some
reason to distrust your government, Mr. Callahan?"

"Not when government officers identify themselves," I said. "Wouldn't it be fair to say that
neither of us has acted properly in this case?"

He lifted his glass. "Touché! I grew up with
two black-sheep cousins. One of them became a
private investigator and the other one an attorney for the mob. I may be biased. This is good
whiskey."

"Thank you."

"You probably think of me as overly secretive," he said. "That doesn't mean I distrust you. I wouldn't tell Rosalynn Carter why I'm in your town, or why we have so much interest in the death of your friend."

"He wasn't that close a friend. I hadn't seen him for years until the day he posted bond for my wife."

"Then why are you spending so much time on his murder?"

"Because I hate killers," I said. "Don't you?"

"Mr. Callahan, it has to be more than that."

"Probably. Joe was in the same business I was. It's not a business that gets any respect from the police or you Washington boys. I don't want his killer to bank on that."

"Did you know him when he was involved in that Scarlatti kidnapping?"

"I knew him. But as I said, I was never his close friend. I have an idea Scarlatti pulled Joe's name at random out of the phone book."

"Maybe," he said, "and maybe not. Is there any more of this bourbon?"

Lunch was big steaming bowls of New England clam chowder, plus grilled Jack cheese and bacon sandwiches on sourdough bread. The sun was out and the day hot when I walked with Delamater to the dark blue Chev he had rented.

At the car, he said "If you learn anything—"

"You and Vogel will be the first to know," I lied.

Their interest in me probably had been based on the belief that I was carrying on for Joe the investigation that troubled them. Bernie probably had assured them that wasn't true. Delamater had braved the storm to decide for himself.

There were other federal agents in town but I hadn't spotted any of them. If the Pinto was their symbol of the intimidation stage, Romolo and I seemed to be the major targets of it. That would mean Joe had been. If Romolo's stooges had found Joe already murdered when they got there. . . .

Don't pursue that thought, Callahan. The Feds may entrap politicians, harass social dissidents, install legally doubtful wiretaps, keep secret files on all citizens who are not registered Republicans. But murder?

No! Not yet. Well, maybe the C.I.A. . . .

Intimidation— What could that mean? That they were trying to frighten Tony Romolo? Harass him? Drive him out of town? Why? Everybody has to be somewhere. Tony was no more of a menace to San Valdesto than he would be to any other place he lived.

The police had their files and their informers. The government men had those and more. They had sophisticated electronic detection and observation systems, lawyers who could make deals and accountants who could ferret out phony financial statements. They had the manpower. They had clout.

What I had was a dead-end alley. I also had an aching back from my morning's labor in the rain. I went out and soaked in the Jacuzzi.

I was just starting to enjoy it when Jan came out to tell me Vogel was on the phone.

"The chief just phoned me," he said. "What's this cock-and-bull story about Calvin's brother-in-law being a big wheel in the mob?"

"It sounds like a cock-and-bull story to me. Where did the chief hear that one?"

"From our Washington friends. I suppose they have a tap on Romolo's phone. When he said the man was driving a Mustang—"

"Whoa!" I said. "Back up and go slower. Who said?"

"Tony Romolo," he explained, "has been phoning Miami about some threat he got from down there. Today he phoned again and said some local bill collector in a Mustang had informed him that Calvin's brother-in-law was a hotshot in the Miami mob. When Romolo phoned the collector's number he got the police department, he told the Miami people."

"A bill collector from the police department driving a Mustang? That's really weird."

"Stop it!"

"Okay. I meant to tell you last night, but I forgot." I told him about my dialogue with the stooges, and added, "I wanted them to think Calvin was out of town."

"I see. And what made you pick Miami? Did you know about this threat to Romolo from there?"

"How could I? I simply picked the first hoodlum town that came to mind."

"You'd better stay out of sight, buddy. And keep that car out of sight, too. They play for keeps."

"Look who's talking—the man who called Tony Romolo a crook to his face."

"I'm a cop, you yo-yo. They don't kill cops."

"Bernie, we both know they'd kill the pope if the price was right. By the way, your Mr. X paid me a visit this morning."

"I know," he said. "You lay low, mister. Not that I give a damn about your hide, but Jan would suffer."

I know—he had said. He had known that Delamater was coming to see me. He might have alerted me. Who was working with whom? Drink my good Scotch, you bum, eat Mrs. Casey's fine food. But don't confide in me. I went back to the Jacuzzi, two hundred and eighteen pounds of petulance.

I really had forgotten last night to tell him about my Arroyo Road theatrical performance. As for lying about the phone call from Miami, the reason for that was embarrassment. I didn't want Bernie to learn how adolescent I could be. I wanted him to believe I was a professional, too.

From the rim of the Jacuzzi above me, Jan said, "Could you move that hulking body over a little? There's room for two in there."

I moved over and she slid in next to me. "What were you muttering about?" she asked.

"Bernie. He knew Delamater was coming over this morning. He could have warned me."

"Warned you? What do you mean? Mr. Delamater wasn't coming over to hit you again, was he?"

"Of course not! He came to question me. Shouldn't Bernie have warned me about that?"

"Why? He's a police officer. He doesn't work for you."

"He has been working *with* me. Doesn't friendship count for anything?"

She sighed. "Bernie was a cop long before he met you and he'll probably be a cop until he dies. His first and only duty is to the public he's paid to protect. If he lets a friendship interfere with that, he's a bad cop—and that he'll never be. Grow up, Brock!"

"I'll try," I promised.

## 15

WE WERE BACK in the house playing gin rummy and I was almost two dollars ahead when Stu Engelke phoned. "Nadia told me you confirmed my suspicion that Joseph Puma was employed by the Trinity Investment Company. I have some things I'd like to talk over with you. Are you busy tonight?"

I asked Jan, "Are we doing anything tonight? Stu Engelke has some things he wants to tell me."

"Tell him to bring Nadia," she said. "We have a lot of food left over from last night. Cocktails at six-thirty, potluck to follow."

My guess had been that he wanted to talk about Trinity. When he came, we went out onto the patio with our drinks; the women stayed inside.

He opened with Trinity. "Did you know," he asked, "that the Mead Land Company is a heavy investor?"

I nodded.

"Some of our Hawkshaw accountants have been investigating them. Do you know who runs Mead Land?"

"Tony Romolo," I said.

"Well, you have been busy!" He sipped his drink. I had the feeling he was doubtful about telling me what was on his mind. Finally: "What I planned to tell you next would be great ammunition for CANA. It could also cost me my job."

I said, "I think I could sacrifice CANA if I thought Tony Romolo was going to be a big investor in this town."

"It might not work out to the advantage of either of us. But it might give you a lead into why your friend was murdered."

"That's my number one project."

"I thought so. If this leaks, *I'm* not your source. Have you ever heard of Livorno Investments?"

I shook my head.

"They recently bought a big block of stock in South Coast. I had them checked out. It's a front for Vince Scarlatti."

"Does your board of directors know this?"

He nodded. "I told the chairman."

"What do they plan to do about it?"

"I don't know. I doubt if there is anything they can do about it without damaging our public image. And I doubt if they have cause. It's a free market and Livorno is legally incorporated. But I remembered that Puma once worked for Scarlatti. If he was investigating Trinity . . . ."

"Romolo might have him bumped?"

"That was the thought I had."

"I had the same thought. If it's true, the Feds

can handle it. I sure don't want to go up against the mob."

He smiled. "Like hell you don't!"

"Oh, *want*, sure. What citizen wouldn't want to? But do?" I shook my head. "I enjoy living too much."

He finished his drink. "The way you played, it's hard for me to believe anything would scare you."

"I was hungrier then. Another drink?"

"I thought you'd never ask."

After the potluck, Jan suggested some bridge. "And Nadia will be my partner," I said. "I understand you play my kind of game."

Nadia frowned. "What kind of game is that?"

"He's insulting you," Jan said. "He plays a cheating game."

"I meant aggressive," I explained. "I meant nonsissy."

"That's my game," Nadia admitted. "We'll go down with a bang, not a whimper."

Bridge conventions are for conventional people. Nadia followed my sports theory that the best defense is a confusing offense. It had rarely worked for me at the card table. It did tonight. We had some lucky finesses and Nadia had a sharp talent for the squeeze play. But what made us the eventual winner was more basic—we held the good cards.

Which Jan, the poor loser, pointed out after they had left. "And," she added, "you finally found somebody who understood your bidding."

"That helped," I admitted.

"You like her, don't you?"

"I like all feisty people. That's one of the reasons I married you."

"Never forget that. You are married to me."

The rain woke me around one o'clock. I went to the window and saw the outside lights go on in front of the houses on our block. The rain was only a drizzle. It stopped before two and the lights went out again.

If you don't mind floods, fires, earthquakes, crazy cults, hoodlums and real-estate agents, California is a nice place to live.

Jan made our breakfast. That was one condition of employment Mrs. Casey had demanded. She did windows but she didn't make breakfasts.

I drove her to ten o'clock Mass at St. Jude's. "You've left the church, Mr. Callahan?" she asked on the way.

"The building," I said. "Not the teaching. I try to follow the teaching of the sisters who educated me."

"And that's enough for you?"

I didn't want to lose this woman. "Not always," I lied.

"My late husband," she said, "hadn't been to Mass for fifteen years before he died. But he asked for a priest on his deathbed."

"I knew two thirty-second-degree Masons who did that."

She sniffed. "Masons? You're not a Mason?"

"No way!"

She sighed. "Well, that's something—"

When I dropped her off, I handed her a twenty. "Put this in the poor box for me."

"Bless you! And I'll pray for your soul, Mr. Callahan."

Twenty dollars was a small price to pay for Irish stew. As for the prayer, I would know if it had gone through when I got there. If He hadn't forgiven Lenny, I'd just as soon go somewhere else. If He wasn't tolerant enough to accept Lenny, He wasn't The Man for me.

Thinking of Lenny made me think of Calvin for some reason. If he was due to get cabin fever, yesterday's storm could have precipitated it, up on that isolated perch. I phoned Sloan Hartford when I got home.

"Is he getting restless?" I asked.

"Not yet. He's a hundred and twelve dollars ahead and I have a feeling he's ready for higher stakes."

"If you notice any strange cars around there, you phone the police. If you spot a black Chrysler Cordoba, lock the doors before you phone."

"Brock, I have seventeen assorted firearms up here, including two elephant guns. I'm sure with that arsenal Cal and I can hold off anything smaller than an infantry division."

"But before you start shooting, you phone the police."

"I will."

He was a sportsman and probably still cherished the naive code that the adversary would play fair. If the Mafia had played fair they would have wound up booking two-lira bets in Sicily.

The Lakers were playing the Celtics in Boston that morning and it would be on the tube. I had been looking forward to that showdown all week.

But Jan had other plans for our viewing pleasure, a PBS program from the same Boston area.

The Union of Concerned Scientists was telecasting a program from Cambridge. Robert Pollard, the nuclear safety engineer who had called for the shutdown of the nuclear power plant at Three Mile Island *two months* before the terrifying accident there, had some things to tell us.

At the Indian Point nuclear power station near New York City, he told us, there were major defects in the plant's emergency cooling system. The mammoth Zion nuclear plant north of Chicago lacked a safe electrical-control system. In California and other earthquake-prone parts of the country several nuclear power plants with inadequate defenses against earthquakes were running at full power.

As for the nuclear power industry's widely advertised claims that the nation urgently needed nuclear energy, these were the facts: nuclear energy accounted for only thirteen percent of the country's electrical production. The ads never mentioned the fact that the United States now had an *excess* in generating capacity of thirty-three percent. The excess was the reason for our exorbitant electric bills.

"They have to be stopped!" Jan said. "But they won't be, will they?"

"I don't know. I heard that Vince Scarlatti bought a big block of stock in South Coast Electric. If that's the new trend in mob investments, the Concerned Scientists had better look for a place to hide."

Something in my unconscious stirred when I said "hide." What? My instinct was trying to tell me something. Was it about Calvin? He was hiding. Had Calvin told me all he knew?

"The bastards!" Jan said. "The greedy bastards!"

If the greedy bastards teamed up with the Mafia guns. . . .

One of my Long Beach homilies came to mind. Change what you can, my father had advised me, and learn to live with what you can't change.

It wasn't a maxim it would be wise to voice to Jan at the moment. I waited until she had gone out to check the storm's erosion in her flower beds before turning on the last two quarters of the Lakers' game.

My Lakers really whomped those overrated Celtics. We had rules of play in my world. There were still some minor satisfactions in my world. The good guys quite often came out on top.

I had used Jan's car to take Mrs. Casey to church. I used it again to pick her up. On the way back I stopped at Thrifty Rental and picked out a blue Chev that duplicated the one Delamater had rented.

I would keep the Mustang out of sight for a few days. I gave them a deposit and told them to deliver the Chev to my house tomorrow. There were a lot of Mustangs in town but not another one with the Spelke logo emblazoned in bright red on the hood.

Dark clouds started to move in again from the Pacific early in the afternoon. I went out with the neighbors to widen our drainage trenches, to pile more sandbags along the banks of the main channel.

The media people loved to dwell on the figures, how many million dollars of property was destroyed in a fire or a flood, how many lives were lost. This was more than mere property; these were our homes.

Ridge Road, high above us, had suffered the most damage. But at the other end of it, where Sloan Hartford lived, the ground was rockier and last winter's fire had not destroyed the ground cover. If he had grown up in that house, it must have gone through dozens of storms.

The rain was light at two o'clock, but growing heavier. The radio informed us that the lowland that bordered Arroyo Road was now flooded. The waterfront homes at the far end of it were on higher ground with a concrete flood-control channel that should keep them safe.

Arroyo Road, however, was the only access to those homes. The residents were advised to stock up on groceries and the other necessities they might need for a few days. Another tropical storm was forty miles off the coast and heading our way.

There was no further digging we could do until the storm came and the flow of water revealed our problem areas. We filled some more bags, stacked them, and went into our homes to wait.

At four o'clock I was in the shower, turning my body red in hot water. The word *hide* kept bugging me. And intimidation? What had Delamater meant by that?

Damn it! I had never been Phi Beta Kappa but my instincts had been more reliable before I retired. Merlin Olsen, our most distinguished Ram, had made Phi Beta Kappa at Utah. Maybe I should phone him.

Phone, phone—another stirring in the unconscious. Key words to be linked, or mental gas?

Calvin's house was in that lowland. He probably didn't own it and it was doubtful that he had anything of value stored there except for his jugs of liquid lightning. Stay where you are, Calvin. Drink some good whiskey for a change and learn to handle an elephant gun.

Twelve years in Vegas and he hadn't learned to fear the mob until now. In a public bar he had mouthed off about a car with Nevada plates he had seen at the site of a murder.

I was in the bedroom dressing when Jan came to the doorway. "You're doing a lot of muttering lately."

"I know."

"Cheer up! The rain has stopped. Maybe the weatherman was wrong again."

He had been. The sun came out before it went down. The radio informed me that the tropical storm we had feared had been diverted to the east and south of us and was now flooding Los

Angeles. The Topanga Canyon road had been washed out. Two homes in the hills above Malibu had already torn loose from their foundations and been completely demolished.

The storm had set an all-time rainfall record for May in Los Angeles. Ninety-five percent of it had fallen in the last three days and it was still coming down.

The eleven o'clock news from there was mostly devoted to disaster scenes and the weather report. Sports had two minutes, world news less.

"Remember my little home in Beverly Glen?" Jan asked.

"I'll never forget it. That's where I lost my virginity."

"Not while I lived there. I'll bet it's leaning now."

"If it's still standing."

"Let's go to bed," she said.

"And pretend we're back in your little house in Beverly Glen?"

"Why not?" she asked.

## 16

I WAS FINISHING a strength-restoring breakfast with a cup of coffee when Sloan Hartford phoned to tell me Calvin had taken off.

"When?"

"Sometime during the night. I didn't hear his car start and I'm a light sleeper. He must have coasted out of the garage and started the engine later. It was a surprise to me. He seemed content."

"Maybe he only went to his house to pick up something or check the rain damage."

"Maybe. That's a crazy dangerous thing to do."

"It's not his first offense. I'll go look for him."

My rented Chev was delivered before I was dressed. I hadn't heard any late reports on the condition of Arroyo Road. It hadn't been closed yesterday when I last heard; it should be closed now.

It was open, but slick with mud from the ploughed fields that bordered it. I drove at a nervous fifteen miles an hour toward Calvin's house.

The front door was open. There was a battered old Dodge pickup truck parked in the driveway.

The gray cat was on the roof of that cab. It jumped off and scooted for the backyard as I drove in.

I was up on the porch when a lanky, bearded old man in chinos and T-shirt appeared in the open doorway with a full gallon jug in each hand.

"Where's Calvin?" I asked him.

He looked at me warily. "Calvin who?"

"Relax. I'm his friend. I'm trying to keep him out of trouble. I'm the man who helped him hide."

"Yeah? What's your name?"

"Callahan, Brock Callahan."

"Let's see your driver's license."

I showed it to him.

"He's at my house," he said. "He was going to phone you later."

"If he lived that long. Where's your house?"

"Follow me," he said.

I followed him to the freeway, down that to the Padero turnoff to lower Main Street. On lower Main, he turned into an alley between a Mexican restaurant and a secondhand-appliance store.

That was what he had called his house, one room and an alcove in the back of the appliance store. The alcove held his bed and a small nightstand.

The room had a gas plate on a shelf, a kitchen table, two kitchen chairs and a faded, sagging velour-covered couch. Calvin was sitting on the couch, reading a girlie magazine. He looked up at me sheepishly when I entered.

"Why?" I asked him.

"I couldn't stand being cooped up in the boon-docks. Besides, he was starting to win."

"And now you're going to leave town?"

"Nah. Who'd find me here?"

"If they want you badly enough they can find you in a comfort station in Tuscaloosa. And now your friend could be in trouble, too."

The bearded man shook his head. "I'm going up north for a while to visit my sister. I won't be around when they waste him."

Calvin snorted. "You guys make me sick!"

"What happened? You were scared silly when you came to my house."

"I told you. I couldn't stand being cooped up. You want your sixty back?"

"Shove it!" I said. "If you were smart, which you aren't, you'd spend it on a bulletproof vest. Calvin, damn it!"

"What you gettin' so steamed about? I'll be here. Anytime you want me, I'll be here. But don't tell Vogel. I don't trust him."

There was no point in arguing with him. It was his neck to do with as he wished. Twelve years in Vegas hadn't taught him a damned thing.

The boys in the Cordoba, the way I saw it, didn't need to protect their own necks. They had their little alibi stooges in El Cajon. They must have suspected that Calvin had seen the earlier action, before they arrived at the lot—the killing of Joe Puma. That's why they were looking for him.

And maybe he had seen it. Who could be sure—

with Calvin? He had hustled his way through a long life, picking up a dollar any way he could. I always wanted to make the majors, he had told Vogel. Maybe he thought he could hit against the big boys and pick up some heavy bread for a change.

He had aroused my anger but not my scorn; he was my kind of hero, a stubborn, gutty loser.

*Hide, phone, intimidation.* There was a pattern in those words somewhere. Currents, crosscurrents and undercurrents—in the swirl of incidents and coincidents there was a pattern trying to emerge.

Banter, threats, chitchat and interrogations—in all that talk there had to be a few lies. But whose and when and why? Some of them obviously had led me down the wrong roads.

I stopped at the police station. Vogel wasn't there. He must have cleaned up his paperwork. I went home. Jan wasn't there. She was starting her first day of labor at Kay Decor Inc.

I phoned Sloan Hartford and told him I'd found Calvin. "He won't be coming back to your house."

"Damn him! Just when I was getting the pattern of his play. I'll miss that little con man. I hope he's in a safe place."

"There are none. Your house weather the storm okay?"

"This place has steel-reinforced concrete pilings thirty feet deep. A typhoon couldn't budge it. If you run into those two who are after Calvin, drag 'em up here and we'll roast 'em over a slow fire."

"That would take some doing. But maybe I can get Vogel up there some night. Thanks for your help."

Almost everybody gambles. Fifty-cent Nassaus or fifty-grand horse bets, Boy Scout lotteries and church bingo games. Everybody gambles but the mob. They don't gamble. They host gamblers, book gamblers, arrange the odds and balance the action so gambling is no game to them. All they do is determine the percentage—and win.

I told Mrs. Casey I wouldn't be home for lunch and went over to the club and hit a bucket of balls on the practice range. When my uncle died and made me a gentleman of leisure, I had planned to play more golf.

Two weeks of daily golf convinced me that was an overindulgence, an opiate for people so limited they couldn't think of anything better to do.

The people I played with now didn't even walk the course. They rode in electric carts. Sloan Hartford could be excused for that—but people with usable legs?

I sweated for half-an-hour in the steam room but didn't stay for lunch. I didn't want to be cornered by some wheelchair athlete who would give me a stroke-by-stroke odyssey of his thrilling eighty-nine.

Joe was dead. Even if the killer was caught and punished, Joe would be just as dead. But men who kill can kill again. Stay with that thought, I told myself.

I had far less equipment than the official

hunters on the same trail. What I had going for me was the fact that people on the shadowed side of the law held an ingrained suspicion of the men who enforced it. Even their stoolies often double-crossed them.

In a country that extols private enterprise, private eyes should get more respect than they do. Dirty jobs are bound to soil the men who work at them. But corrupt them? It was hard for me to believe that about Joe.

At Hanna's Hamburger Heaven I had her cheeseburger, bacon and avocado delight and a pineapple milk shake and considered my next move. I had none.

I had Joe's hieroglyphics and some mental gas that refused to coalesce. I was nowhere. A place I had been before.

It was a nice day for a drive; I drove out to Point Mirage. Three young people and the woman rancher in tennis shoes were the only pickets working this afternoon.

I picked out a sign that read One Hiroshima Is Enough and joined the circling walkers. Each time I passed the bored guard I gave him my most malevolent look. He yawned back at me.

All that had happened had revolved around CANA. Except for Calvin; he was the only person outside the periphery. Even Joey had been involved in CANA. If he hadn't been, I wouldn't have met Joe at the county jail. His wife wouldn't have phoned me. I wouldn't have had my name in his file, probably not gone to visit his widow. That had put the Feds on my trail.

Around and around we plodded, concerned
citizens protesting corporation arrogance. The
big corporations had poisoned our land, stripped
our forests and polluted our rivers and lakes. We
had about as much chance of winning as Woody
Allen would have fighting Ali.

I had been a wheelchair golfer too long. My
feet gave out after an hour and a half.

"Mine, too," the woman rancher told me.
"How would you like to buy me another double
boilermaker?"

"It will be my pleasure. Did Lois introduce us
that day?"

She shook her head. "My name is Stella Robin.
And you're Brock the Rock, aren't you?"

"The same," I said modestly. "Your car or
mine?"

"We'll take both cars," she said. "The bar's
out near my ranch and I can go home from
there."

I followed her dusty Jeep to the Happy Hour
Café, a stained and ancient stucco building near
the lemon growers' cooperative warehouse.

In a booth there, I ordered a double boilermaker for her and a glass of draught beer for me.

"I've been hearing rumors around town," she
told me. "That detective who was killed, was he
investigating the Trinity Investment Company?"

"He was. Barlow told me Puma was working
for him to discredit the rumors of Mafia involvement."

"I'll bet! Barlow is the Trinity Investment Company, isn't he?"

"Most of it."

"Then why haven't the cops picked him up? He proved he was capable of murder years ago."

"Judson Barlow murdered somebody?"

"Not quite. And he was only eighteen at the time. But he really worked another young man over with a tire iron. It was touch and go for that young man for more than a month. Judson's dad got nicked for a quarter-million-dollar settlement."

"I'll remind Lieutenant Vogel," I said. "I've been working with him."

"You do that." She gulped her double shot and washed it down with the small glass of beer. "You probably think I'm pushy, but I needed the boost and I forgot to bring my purse."

"Another?" I asked.

She shook her head. "I have to drink and run. You check out that Barlow. I'd love to see him wind up in the gas chamber."

I used the wall phone to call the station. Vogel was there. I relayed the information she had given me.

"He was checked yesterday," Bernie said. "If we can believe his wife, his alibi is sound."

Calvin had asked me not to tell Vogel where he was. But somebody had to keep an eye on him. I related the morning's adventure from Hartford's phone call to the lower Main Street finals.

"I think," he said, "it's time to put that bum into protective custody. I'll have him picked up."

His voice was weary and dispirited. He had a depressing job. The only solid citizens he met in his daily grind were either dead or defrauded. That had to make a man cynical.

Sociologists can philosophize about the causes of crime, poverty, ignorance, an abused childhood. Vogel had to deal with the results. His was the real world, not the academic.

His duty was to maintain a world orderly enough to afford the academics the freedom to philosophize.

Jan was home when I got there, all charged up about her first day back in harness. "Audrey offered me a salary," she explained, "but I think straight commission would be fairer for her, wouldn't it?"

"I agree. Let the customer carry the load."

"You're sour, aren't you?"

"Nope. Audrey Kay's customers are not poor. They must be accustomed to big markups by now. And they can well afford it."

"You're sour. Bad day?"

"Frustrating. I'm sure whatever you decide, you won't cheat Audrey and she won't cheat you."

A Casey dinner brought me partway back to a reasonable frame of mind. An hour after dinner, a phone call from Ellen Puma brought me the rest of the way. She had landed the job with the young lawyer.

Joe was dead but his widow had a job and his son would be going to law school.

And then, as lagniappe to an improving day,

PBS offered us *Hamlet* that night with a cast almost worthy of it. My favorite play, about the all-time noblest, flakiest loser in the literary world.

**17**

STRETCHING AND TURNING, trying to sleep. It wouldn't come. Lower Main Street would be buzzing now with small-time hookers and gamblers and thieves on the prowl. For a ten spot or a fix, the boys in the Cordoba could buy some poor wretch who could find Calvin for them. Damn him!

At two o'clock I got up and drank a glass of warm milk. At three o'clock I was back in bed. At eight-thirty Jan wakened me to tell me Vogel was on the phone.

I knew what he was going to tell me. I picked up the phone and said, "He's dead, isn't he?"

"Who's dead?"

"Calvin."

"Where'd you hear about it?"

"I didn't. I just knew. I thought you were going to put him under protective custody?"

"We couldn't find him. He wasn't there when the officer went to his friend's house. He was found up near the reservoir, wringing wet. They must have thought he would drown. Two broken arms, internal bleeding and a concussion. Officially, he's dead."

"What do you mean?"

"He's in intensive care at Loreli General."

"You mean he can testify against those creeps?"

"If he ever regains consciousness, which is doubtful right now. I shouldn't have told you this. If it leaks, you'll join Calvin. We want those two to stay in town."

"You think Calvin hasn't learned his lesson after what they did to him? Would you testify against them after that?"

"Probably not. I'm not Calvin. And if he lives, Uncle Sam can make it worth his while. They can set him up in a whole new life."

Nothing from me.

Vogel said, "The Feds are sending in reserves. F.B.I. this time. Enough for twenty-four-hour watches. They'll break this thing."

"Sure."

"And we never had this conversation. Is that clear?"

"Yes."

"What the hell are you so down about? This is our big break."

"I've had a bad night. I'll see you later, Bernie."

This is our big break.... Not to Calvin. The hoods had given him his breaks, one in each arm. Had they found him, I wondered, or had he tried to hustle them? He couldn't be that dumb.

Oh, yes, he could. He was kookier than Hamlet. Maybe guttier.

"What was that all about?" Jan asked.

"Bernie wants to play poker with Sloan Hartford."

"You're lying," she said.

"Possibly. Have you eaten?"

"Of course. I have to be in the shop in ten minutes."

She left. Mrs. Casey, who didn't make breakfasts, suggested a nice cheese-and-ham omelet for me.

While Calvin was probably getting his nourishment through needles in his veins, I ate a delicious omelet. I should have felt guilty about that. I felt guilty about not feeling guilty. The damned fool!

Joe and Calvin, losers both, trying to hustle the mob? Maybe Calvin, but Joe hadn't been that dumb. So far as I knew, Joe had worked *for* a mobster in his only contact with them.

So far as I knew, but what did I know? Something that resembled a pattern was starting to take shape in my foggy brain. The dawn wasn't here but a clouded line of inquiry was starting to form.

On the investigative trail CANA had acted as a partial diversion. I was almost sure of that. This was mob business first, ecology concern second.

It would take a C.P.A. superman to discover all the businesses in America in which the mob was involved. It would not be unreasonable to guess there was not a profitable field of enterprise in our economy in which they were not obviously or secretly involved. That was why the Feds had come to town. The San Valdesto police force couldn't bat in that league.

As Vogel had said—nobody cares. Our most admired theatrical stars play the hoodlum casinos, luring the square solid citizens to Vegas. This gives the mob enough money to put the squares' kids on heroin.

I knew the administrative head at Loreli General, a high-handicap hacker. I phoned him and asked him how Calvin was doing.

"If you mean Calvin Ellers, he's dead."

"Officially? Or actually? If you doubt my credentials, you can phone Lieutenant Vogel."

"I have never doubted your credentials, Brock, only your handicap. He's still alive. Our chief of staff told me half an hour ago any patient less stubborn would have been dead when they found him."

"Is he conscious?"

"Not yet. The current medical prognosis is that he never will be."

"Don't bet on it," I said. "And thanks."

They probably had assumed he was dead. They had broken both arms, tore up his insides, rendered him unconscious and thrown him into the reservoir. What else could they assume?

Killing him hadn't been their original objective probably. All they wanted from him was something he didn't know—who had killed Joe Puma? Hoodlums can never accept the possibility that somebody might be telling the truth. Honesty is alien to their world.

They had been at the scene of the crime and not reported it. A lawyer would know if that was illegal; I didn't. So far as I knew, there was no law that forced a man to become a citizen. Calvin might have thought it was illegal and tried to profit from it.

I looked up Park Livett's office number and dialed it. Ellen answered.

"Busy?" I asked her.

"Not yet. But we will be. He's a very bright young man. And I'll never be too busy for you."

"I had this thought that maybe the five hundred Joe got every Christmas could be a retainer. Is it possible he could still have been working for Vince Scarlatti?"

"Certainly not for Vince. He's in a state of advanced senility in a Beverly Hills sanitarium. I think that check from Peter is pure gratitude. The way Joe told it to me, he had a hard time convincing those kidnappers that Peter should go home alive."

"Were the kidnappers ever caught?"

"Never."

"Does Peter live in Beverly Hills, too?"

"No. I have his address at home. I thought the least we could do is send him a Christmas card. He lives in that subdivision with all those Italian street names on the cliff above the Riviera Country Club."

"That's in Pacific Palisades?"

"It is. Did you plan to visit him?"

"Not without a good reason. I wondered if maybe you could phone him and tell him I'm working for you?"

"I haven't his phone number and there's no way I could get it. I could write you a letter of recommendation. I'll tell him what I think of you. There'll be no need to lie."

"I'd appreciate that. I'll pick it up, and the address, in a day or so. My favorite aunt is in the hospital and I don't want to leave town until she's better."

"I'm sure you wouldn't," she said. "I'll get it all ready for you."

It might work. It might not. If Peter had inherited his father's insular vindictive personality, it wouldn't. Vince would never have sent Christmas gifts to an employee already paid. That must have started when Peter took over the reins.

Thy name is Peter and on this rock I build my case. . . .

Ellen had said she didn't have his number. What about that number I had tried and been told it didn't exist? It probably was not a San Valdesto number.

I rummaged through the papers and found the slip. The initials were D.D. David Delamater was the only person I'd met in this case with those initials. They weren't Peter's.

What did I have to lose? I dialed one and two-one-three and the number. A crisp feminine voice answered, "Dr. Darius's office."

"Is this," I asked, "the Dr. Darius who lives in Sherman Oaks?"

"No, sir. I've never heard of him. Are you sure of the address?"

"I think so. Where is your office?"

"In Santa Monica, where Dr. Darius has lived most of his life."

"It can't be the same man," I told her. "You're sure there is no other Dr. Darius?"

"I have no idea. Was there another one in the phone book?"

"I'll look," I said. "Thank you."

Half an hour later Vogel phoned to tell me the Feds had changed their story and their strategy. Calvin was no longer officially dead, only missing.

"Why?" I asked.

"If those two hoods read that he's dead, they'll know we'll be picking them up for questioning. If they think he's at the bottom of the reservoir and they're the only ones who know it, they'll be more likely to stay in town."

"I suppose by now you've checked the priors on those two?"

"Delamater has. They're a pair of brothers out of Detroit. They rented the Chrysler in Vegas. Both of them have been charged and acquitted of murder twice—when witnesses changed their testimony or disappeared. Both have served time for assault."

"Do they have names?"

"Why do you want to know?"

"Because I'm working on this case, too. If you want me to quit, say the word."

"No macho crap, Brock."

"I'm not that brave or that dumb."

"Their names are Rodney and Arvid Patulski."

Rodney and Arvid? They sounded like a comedy team. I put their names on the list along with Dr. Darius. I went through Joe's notes for any

tidbits that might make more sense in the light of
what I'd learned since I had picked them up.
Nothing there. I added some things I'd been told
that needed to be checked. A lie can point a
finger.

All this and the letter from Ellen Puma I would
take with me to the Palisades. With Vince out of
the picture maybe I would get some answers. Or
maybe I would get two broken arms.

I phoned Kay Decor, hoping that Jan would go
to lunch with me. She was, I was told, up in
Solvang with a client. Not a customer, you
understand, a client. If the shop had been called
Thrifty Furnishings, it would have been a customer.

I told Mrs. Casey I wouldn't be home for lunch
and drove in my blue Chev to Loreli General. The
high-handicap hacker there told me the last he
had heard, Calvin was still unconscious. He
called intensive care to make sure. Calvin was
still unconscious.

From there to the one-room-and-alcove home
of Calvin's bearded friend. Nobody answered my
knock on his door. His landlord, the store owner,
told me his tenant was out of town visiting his
sister.

I was safely back in the Chev, heading the
other way, when the black Cordoba came down
Main Street and turned into the alley.

No macho crap, Brock.... But the urge was
strong. How could a whole man be afraid of a
pair named Rodney and Arvid? Oh, Rodney, oh,
Arvid, if you didn't have friends with guns,

Sloan Hartford and I right now would be roasting you both over a slow fire.

I stopped at the station to tell Vogel I had seen the black car turn into the alley. I told him they would find nothing there; Calvin's friend was out of town.

"I know. You going to take me to lunch at Pierre's?"

"What have you got against Big Macs and French fries? I feel uncomfortable around food you can't put catsup on."

"Okay, cheapskate, forget it."

We went to Pierre's in the rented Chev. On the way, I told him about my plan to visit Peter Scarlatti.

"Why? What can you learn that a zillion federal cops can't?"

"Mrs. Puma is on my side, not theirs. That's my edge. What can we lose? I'm not costing the taxpayers a dime."

"You can get your dumb head blown off."

"I didn't know you cared, Bernie."

"I don't. But if they bump you, who takes me to Pierre's?"

When I dropped him off at the station two hours later, and forty-three dollars poorer, there was no place to go but home. Which is where I went.

## 18

THE CAPITAL-PUNISHMENT ADVOCATES love to link crime with murder in their sales pitches to their vindictive followers. The fact is that more than two-thirds of the country's murders are committed by citizens without previous criminal records. Drunken drivers claim many more victims than murderers year after year.

Capital punishment might be a deterrent to drivers inclined to take one more for the road. The gas chamber should scare them more than losing their drivers' licenses. A cuckolded husband or violent bar brawler is not likely to be thinking about the gas chamber in his rage.

Mob killings, that's a different story. They account for a very small percentage of the nation's homicides. The rub is that they are the ones that most often go unsolved or unpunished. Some are unsolved because they aren't reported. The victims simply disappear. If they are solved, the killers too often are acquitted. Because the witnesses disappear.

Rodney and Arvid were still cruising the town, banking on the premise that their combined victim-witness had disappeared. I hoped they hadn't learned about Calvin's previous Ridge Road sanctuary. Or learned the address of the bearded man's sister.

I phoned Vogel and alerted him to the possibility. "They inquired," he told me. "They didn't learn anything because the store owner didn't know the address."

"I've been thinking about Sloan Hartford—"

"That's being covered," he said in his too patient voice. "Any more advice?"

"Burn your leisure suit," I said, and hung up.

There was an ache between my shoulder blades and another starting in my skull. I took two aspirin, put on my trunks and went out to the Jacuzzi.

Vogel had said the Feds could be our last best hope. Peter Scarlatti could be mine. The Feds and I had different goals. They were trying to discover whatever shenanigans Joe had been involved in. I was trying to find his killer.

I phoned my Loreli friend before he went home. The latest word on Calvin was that he was still unconscious. But the prognosis was better. There was now a remote possibility that he would live.

Jan didn't look happy when she came home. She had forgotten how difficult some clients—customers—could be, she told me.

I made her a drink and listened sympathetically to her detailed lament. "So you started with a lemon," I said soothingly. "Your next client could be a big payoff."

"Oh, this woman will come around," she told

me. "What annoyed me was her superior attitude. She hasn't the slightest idea how vulgar her taste is."

"Concentrate on how green her money is," I said, "and consider what a favor you're doing her by refining her taste."

"I'll concentrate on her money. Her taste is hopeless."

My Jan had rejoined me in the real world.

Calvin was still unconscious in the morning. I phoned Ellen before she went to work. She had the letter and the address for me. I could pick them up at her house in the next half hour.

"That's too soon for me. I'll pick them up at your office."

At breakfast, I told Jan I might be out of town for a few days.

"Out of town where—and why?"

"The Santa Monica area. The Palisades, maybe Venice. I have to see some people."

"Business?" she asked.

I nodded.

"Is Bernie going with you?"

I shook my head.

"You don't want to tell me about it?"

"I'd rather not."

"It's dangerous, isn't it?"

"I doubt it. I'm going to visit the friend of a friend, one of Joe Puma's benefactors. It might take only a day."

"You can't quit working, can you?"

I smiled at her.

"Oh, shut up!" she said.

Before she left, she made me promise that I would phone her if I stayed longer than a day. I promised. It would take longer than a day. I packed some clothes and got some money at the bank before I stopped in at Livett's office.

"Luck," Ellen said. "And you be careful. Watch your tongue. Joe told me you have a nasty tongue."

I was reading the letter. "You didn't mention it in here. Don't you think you made me a little nicer than I am?"

She shook her head. "And if Peter wants confirmation, you'll notice my home and office phone numbers are in the letter."

I took the Chev. Like Delamater, I had left the intimidation stage and was now in the investigative. Normally, I would have taken the coast road at Oxnard, the most pleasant route to Santa Monica. But the rain had cluttered it with boulders in the Malibu area and sent the clay cliffs of the Palisades sliding down.

I took the freeway to the San Diego turnoff and that to Sunset Boulevard. The sun was out, the traffic heavy. To the right on Sunset, winding toward the ocean.

The Scarlatti home could have been transplanted from the Middle West, right out of Oak Park. It was a two-story place of red brick, on the rim above the golf course. Vince had first come to prominence in Chicago.

The woman who came to the door was dark skinned, gray haired and middle-aged. Peter, she told me, was out on the course, his first chance to

play golf in two weeks. She didn't know when he
would be home.

I gave her the letter. "Will he be home around
dinnertime? I could phone him then."

"He has an unlisted number," she said, "and
I'm not supposed to give it out."

"I'm almost sure," I told her, "that he'll see
me after he reads the letter. Would it be all right
if I came back after dinner?"

"I don't know. You could try. I'll give him the
letter."

I took Sunset back to the nearest place I could
cut through to San Vicente Boulevard and that to
Santa Monica. I didn't stop in Santa Monica.

Two blocks beyond its border, the Venice office of Tracy Perlman Investigations was on the
second floor of a two-story frame building, above
a liquor store.

I was going up the steps of his office as he came
down. Gad, he looked old. He had always been
skinny; now he looked shriveled.

"Callahan," he said. "For Christ's sake! First
Puma, and now you. What the hell's going on up
there in San Valdesto?"

"Puma was here?"

"Three weeks ago. And now he's dead. What
happened?"

"That's what I'm trying to find out. Could we
talk?"

"I'm going to lunch. We can talk if you'll buy."

"You name the place," I said, "and I'll pick up
the tab."

He named the place, Antoine's, only a little

more expensive than Pierre's. As we climbed into the Chev he asked doubtfully, "Are you sure you can afford Antoine's?"

"It's a rental car, Trace. I was afraid to bring the Rolls down here into this crummy neighborhood. What did Joe want with you?"

"I'll tell you after my first martini. Is it true what I heard, that you inherited a wad?"

"More or less. You wouldn't gouge a fellow investigator, would you, Trace?"

He sighed. "Brock the Rock, as sarcastic as ever."

The parking attendant at Antoine's looked skeptically at the Chev and then at Trace, but made no comment. The maître d' found us a small, secluded table, well screened from most of his other diners.

I ordered a martini for Trace and a glass of draught Einlicher for me and gave the waiter the haughtiest eye I could achieve.

"How's business?" I asked Trace.

"I eat. Not here, of course. One more year and I've had it. I'll be sixty-four next month."

He looked eighty. I said nothing.

"Bought me a trailer home in Hemet," he said. "Got a nephew there, my sister's boy. He's got a gas station and I can pick up enough on part-time work there."

"What did Joe want?"

"Some information about a Santa Monica doctor named Darius. Joe figured Santa Monica was my stamping grounds."

"Who knows it better than you?"

"Raymond Chandler, maybe. But he called it Bay City. Anyway, I gave him what I had and he gave me a double sawbuck. Then, two weeks later, I read he got wasted up in your town. Mafia, Brock?"

I shrugged.

He took a deep breath and a sip of his martini. "They're all over, aren't they?"

"I guess. Another martini?"

"Why not? All I had on Darius was the name of his girl friend. What Joe found out from her I don't know."

"Darius is married?"

"Oh, yes. Real solid citizen. Gets a lot of the movie trade, big-money people."

I signaled the waiter, ordered two more of the same. When he went away, I asked, "What's Darius's speciality?"

"Cosmetic surgery."

That could be the link. Hide, phone, intimidation; the pattern was forming. I said, "And you're going to sell me the name of the girl friend, aren't you?"

"Hell, man, I'd give it to you free. This meal is going to cost you more than Joe paid me. But I ain't about to go up against the mob, Brock. Even pumping gas is better than being dead. That Puma had more brass than sense."

The waiter brought our menus and we ordered the specialty of the day, fresh mountain trout.

"Those damned Rams," Trace said, "moving to Anaheim. After all the money they made in L.A. No loyalty anymore, is there?"

"Not much."

"Who you working for, Brock?"

"Myself. Nobody's paying me. I just don't want Joe's death to go unnoticed. He's one of ours, Trace."

"I suppose. But I'd hate to get knocked off in my last year in the game."

"Has it been a game to you?"

"Mostly. It's mean at times, sure. It's still better than bucking rivets at Douglas or driving a bus. I could have worked for one of the big agencies. But, hell, I was always my own man."

That he was, without wife or kids. He would wind up living in a trailer in Hemet, working part-time in a gas station to pad out his Social Security. Call it the Sam Spade syndrome; dreamers, all of us.

We ate our trout, finished with Turkish coffee and went back to his office. It was small and shabby but it was clean. Trace had always been neat.

He took a slim file out of his cabinet. "I got her grounds for divorce," he said, tapping the file. "Later, some punk kid tried to blackmail her. He was threatening to tell Darius's wife about their love nest. I scared him off. You don't plan to play it heavy with her, do you, Brock?"

"Have I ever?"

"I don't know. I never followed you that close. What I mean, she's a real nice lady who was married to a creep and she's been the doc's faithful back-street wife for six years."

Her name was Mary Bettis. She lived on Ocean

Avenue. It was a small apartment, he explained, over the garage behind the main house. She was probably at work now.

I took out my wallet and said, "Thanks, Trace. I'll walk softly."

"Put your money away," he said. "You're right. Joe was far from being a saint but he was one of ours."

I didn't insist. He really was his own man.

I drove over to the San Vicente Lodge and rented a room. I phoned Mary Bettis from there. Nobody answered. I phoned Kay Decor, Inc., in San Valdesto and Jan was there.

"It will be at least one night," I told her. "The people I have to talk with aren't home during the day."

"Okay. I think I have Madame Vulgar Taste ready to sign."

"I was sure you would. Hang in there, tiger. I'm at the San Vicente Lodge." I gave her the phone number. "If anybody wants me up there, they can leave a message."

Then I phoned my friend at Loreli General. Calvin was still unconscious. The prognosis was still as bleak as the last one he had given me.

The black clouds started to drift in from the ocean around four o'clock. It was misty outside at five, drizzling at six.

Peter Scarlatti had got his golf in before the rain had returned. That should put him in a good mood.

## 19

THE RAIN never got really heavy, only nasty. The vagrant wind kept blowing it from one direction and then another. The Chev moved through it undaunted along the winding road called Sunset Boulevard.

Parked on Peter Scarlatti's driveway was one magnificent car, possibly the finest this country has every produced. It was a gleaming black Duesenberg roadster with Dayton wire wheels, including a spare wheel mounted in each front-fender well.

I stood in the rain, getting wet and staring. I was still standing there when the light went on next to the front door.

A broad, fairly short man stood on the porch. "Mr. Callahan?" he called.

"Yes." I turned to face him. "Is that a 1933 J?"

"S.J. Did you come here to talk about cars?"

I walked up under the protection of the porch. "No. It's just that I've wanted one of those for ten years. Is it for sale?"

"No." He held out a hand. "I'm Peter Scarlatti." I shook his hand.

"Unless," he said, "you have a loose quarter of a million dollars you'd like to throw away?"

"If that's a firm price, you've got a deal."

"Cash?"

"Cash. I can have it here as soon as the bank opens tomorrow."

He smiled. "It's not for sale. Come in."

We walked through a dimly lighted living room and along an unlighted hall to a book-lined study at the rear of the house.

He indicated a chair in there and I sat down. He stood for a few seconds, studying me. "Were you joking? If you weren't, you must be doing a lot better in your trade than Joe did."

"Not much. I'm not in the trade anymore. I had a rich uncle. He drove his Ferrari into a bridge abutment one night—and I retired."

"You mean this work you're doing for Mrs. Puma is charity?"

"Yes. You see, Joe. . . . Well, no matter what he was, he was one of ours. Can you understand that?"

He smiled again. "Of course."

This was no slick Tony Romolo in tennis shorts. This was a square, solid, old-country son carrying on the family business.

"My father bought that S.J.," he told me, "from Augie Duesenberg forty-seven years ago. It's been in the family ever since. Drink, Mr. Callahan?"

"Bourbon and water, thank you."

He went to the liquor cabinet behind his desk and made a pair of them. He brought mine over and went to sit behind the desk.

"How long," he asked, "has Tony been up in your town?"

"I'm not sure. A couple of months. He has a heavy investment, I understand, in the land around that projected nuclear plant at Point Mirage. A professor at the university up there is the majority stockholder."

"You think Tony might be responsible for what happened to Joe?"

"I don't know. I hope not. I don't want to go up against him."

He nodded. "He's crazy! He should be driving the Duesy. He's still living in the thirties."

"Maybe in the nineteenth century. He even has a butler."

"He would. It's very important to third-class people to live first-class. What do you want from me, Mr. Callahan?"

"Whatever crumbs you might throw my way. I don't want to go up against you, either."

His ever-ready smile again. "I've watched you play. I'm sure I don't frighten you. You must have some theories about what happened."

"There were a couple of boys, who might have been working for Tony, that the police have questioned. Brothers. Rodney and Arvid Patulski. Have you heard of them?"

He nodded.

"But they have five people ready to swear they were in El Cajon the night Joe was killed."

"And the police bought that?"

"I don't know. They don't confide in me completely."

"How about the Feds? They're up there, too, aren't they?"

I nodded.

He took a deep pull from his glass. "Say what you think. Ask what you want. You're certified."

I took a swallow of liquid courage and said, "I was wondering about that five hundred you send the Pumas. I was thinking it might be a retainer. Maybe Joe had a line on those men who kidnapped you. Maybe they're in San Valdesto."

He shook his head. "If Joe was looking for them, he'd need a spade. Is that frank enough?"

"It is. And you never said it. So that takes us back to the power plant." I paused for another sip of courage booster. "Is it true one of your corporations has a big block of stock in the South Coast Electric Company?"

"Which corporation?"

"Livorno Investments."

"I honestly don't know. That was only set up a few months ago. But I'll find out for you tomorrow morning. My investment counselor is coming back from Chicago later tonight. What's your angle there?"

"It would put Tony on the opposite side of the fence from you again. Joe was investigating the company that owns the land around the plant. The professor told me he had hired him—but I'm not sure I believe him."

He was silent, apparently considering his next words. Then: "There's an angle you may be overlooking. I want to talk with some—with some of my associates before I mention it. Will you still be in town tomorrow?"

I nodded. "At the San Vicente Lodge in Santa Monica."

"They'll probably go along with me," he said. "But who can ever be sure? I inherited a complicated business and it's not possible to completely desert it. I heard yesterday that Tony is in trouble with his Miami friends. I don't want to make his mistake."

"I understand. You've been more cooperative than I had a right to expect."

"Joe saved my life," he said. "I pay my debts."

The rain had stopped, the stars were out. Maybe the dawn would come.

There had been an angle I had overlooked, but not anymore. Joe hadn't been working for Barlow. Barlow had lied to us. The bull probably knew more about the Mead Land Company, or suspected more, than he was ready to admit.

It was still early. I drove to the address Tracy had given me. The address was for the big house, the only house on the block, sandwiched between towering apartment buildings. The apartment over what Tracy had called a garage was served by an alley that ran behind the house and the apartment buildings.

It wasn't a garage; it was a double carport under her apartment. There was a Chevette hatchback in the carport and a Cadillac DeVille. The doctor and his back-street wife might be sharing a cozy late supper; it would be bad manners to disturb them now.

I left a wake-up call for seven and phoned Mary Bettis at seven-thirty. I explained to her that I was a private consultant working with the San Valdesto Police Department investigating the murder of a man named Joseph Puma.

"What does that have to do with me?"

"We found your name in his files. And another local resident, a Dr. Darius. Do you know him?"

"I think," she said, "I had better phone the San Valdesto Police Department before I answer any more questions."

"If you wish. But don't talk with anybody else up there but Lieutenant Vogel. The Justice Department has asked us to keep this investigation as private as possible. That's why I was hired."

"You're working with the Justice Department, too?"

"With only one of their agents, a man named David Delamater. As I said, this is not a case where many officers are involved. In police departments, even in the Justice Department, there are leaks. And we certainly don't want any more murders. Would it be possible for me to meet you for lunch? At our expense, of course."

"All right. I guess I can wait until after that to phone San Valdesto."

"It might be wise. Joseph Puma had a lot of connections and some very unsavory associates."

"I can believe that. In front of Caldwell Savings and Loan at noon?"

"I'll be there. And thank you for your trust."

I went down to the dining room well pleased

with myself. The muscle days were behind me; suavity was my new approach.

A glass of orange juice, four eggs, six pork-sausage links, three rolls and two cups of coffee later, I picked up the *Times* in the lobby and went back to the room.

I had finished the financial pages, the sports, skimmed the world news and was deep in the prose of Jack Smith when my phone rang.

Peter Scarlatti said, "Could you come here? I don't like to talk over the phone."

"I'm on the way."

The swarthy housekeeper answered the door and led me to the study. There was another man in there with Peter, a slim man of medium height, wearing horn-rimmed glasses and a conservative vested suit.

I was not introduced to him. Nor did either man suggest I sit down. We all remained standing.

"This angle I mentioned last night," Peter said, "is only a rumor and I have no idea how sound it is. There is a possibility, though, that Joe was looking for a man named Lester Hardin. Have you ever heard of him?"

I shook my head.

"He was the major witness for the Justice Department when they put Nick Romolo away. He was the man who clinched the case for them."

"And you think he's in San Valdesto?"

Peter shrugged.

"How about the Patulski brothers? Do they work for Tony?"

"They seem to be working for him now. They

work for anybody who needs their kind of work to be done." He paused. "As for that big block of stock in the South Coast Electric Company, one of my corporations held five hundred shares—which we sold this morning. I've never favored utility stocks. Five hundred shares would hardly constitute a big block, as I understand the term. Anything else?"

"Not unless you want to sell the Duesy?"

"No way." His smile again. "Let me say, before you leave, that I think you were even better than Merlin Olsen."

"No way," I said. "But thanks for the thought and your help."

CANA had been a diversion. Oh, what a tangled web we weave when first we practice to deceive.... Honest men should not practice it. It takes years of training. He had tried to lead me down all the wrong trails—and trapped himself.

I knew, as you must know by now. I didn't want to know. I didn't want to meet Mary Bettis to make sure.

Maybe I was wrong. It wouldn't be the first time. At noon I was standing in front of the Caldwell Savings and Loan office.

A woman came out a few minutes after noon. She was not the pallid prototype of the suffering second woman. She was tanned, she was slim. She was smartly dressed in a camel-hair skirt and a tan suede jerkin over a cream-colored silk blouse.

"Mr. Callahan?" she asked.

"Yes. Dr. Livingstone, I presume?"

"Please! It's the wrong time for low comedy. Are you the Brock Callahan who played football?"

"Yes."

"My brother thinks you're God."

"Let's talk about lunch. Antoine's?"

She shook her head. "I haven't that much time. There's a sandwich shop around the corner where the food is almost edible."

We got there before the line formed. She ordered a bacon-and-tomato sandwich on toast; I ordered a double cheeseburger.

She said crisply, "I phoned Dr. Darius from the office. He'll see you tonight, at my place."

"You know him?"

"Don't be devious, Mr. Callahan. You know I know him, just as Mr. Puma did. That was his sword. He might be your friend, but I'll say it anyway. I'm glad he's dead."

I said nothing.

"Was he a friend of yours?"

I shook my head.

"You didn't know him?"

"I knew him. Not well. I used to work down here."

She sniffed.

"Puma," I told her, "was in the same business I used to be in. It's a dirty business. He had a wife to support and a kid he hoped to get into law school. If he turned dirtier than the rest of us—" I shrugged.

"He had cause? Is that what you're trying to say?"

"Let's call it economic pressure. I'm not here to defend him."

"You don't plan to use the same approach, the same wedge?"

"What wedge?"

"Revealing my relationship with Dr. Darius?"

"Of course not! Did Puma threaten to do that?"

"He did."

"I wouldn't. I never have. Is that the only reason Dr. Darius agreed to talk with me?"

"Why else?"

"Because, being a doctor, I had this naive belief that he might share my repugnance for killing and killers. I came down here at my own expense, I've spent a week on this case without fee. You tell your Dr. Darius he doesn't have to talk with me tonight."

Silence while we ate. When our coffee came she said, "My place, tonight at six-thirty."

## 20

THIS HAD NEVER BEEN A WHODUNIT. All the fingers had pointed in the same direction. This had been a whydunit and now I had the why. I should have let the Feds handle it. What business was it of mine? Joe, you bastard! Nobody should ever get that hungry.

I'd had a phone call from San Valdesto, the clerk told me. He took a slip from my box. "A Lieutenant Vogel. He wants you to call him back before three." He handed me the slip.

It was only one-thirty. I phoned him from my room. "What the hell are you doing down there?" he asked me.

"Playing in a member-guest at Riviera Country Club. Why?"

"I'm going to ask you once before I tell the Santa Monica police to pick you up. A Dr. Darius phoned me. I covered for you, as you knew I would. What's your business with him?"

"Ask Delamater. He'll know. I thought they were supposed to be working with us."

"They're all through working. And I'm sure they don't want any peepers messing around in their business. What has Darius got to do with them?''

"You ask Delamater. What do you mean they're through working?''

"Calvin is conscious. They brought those Patulski brothers to his room and he identified both of them. He lied to us. He saw them kill Puma. That old coot was probably trying to blackmail them, but he'll never admit it.''

"And why did they kill Joe?''

"How would I know? That's federal business. Hush-hush stuff. When it's Mafia, I don't want to know. Who is this Darius?''

"He's my partner in the member-guest. We're due to tee off in half an hour. I'll see you tomorrow.''

"Just a minute—'' he said.

I hung up. I called the clerk and told him to get my bill ready; I was checking out.

I was packing when the phone rang. I let it ring. At the desk the clerk said, "Lieutenant Vogel phoned again. I guess you weren't in the room. He wants you to call him back.''

"I've decided to go up there and see him,'' I said. "If he calls again, tell him I'm on the way.''

Maybe he'd believe me and maybe he wouldn't. Either way, I was (almost) sure he wouldn't have me picked up. Not my Bernie buddy. But what if he told Delamater I was seeing Darius? He wouldn't. The case was closed. Bernie wouldn't get me into trouble.

Still there was no reason for me to hang around Santa Monica until six-thirty. I had no friends in town. I drove over to Venice to the office of Tracy Perlman Investigations.

He was in his office, typing out bills on a portable typewriter.

"Did you talk with Mary Bettis?" he asked.

"Yep. Took her to lunch. Have you heard the news from San Valdesto?"

He shook his head.

"The Feds have wrapped it up. A couple of guns out of Detroit killed Joe. Romolo's men, I guess."

"So you wasted a trip?"

"No. I came down to find out why, not who. I almost knew who before I came down."

"You can't take almosts into court."

"Right. Want to go out for a couple of beers? I've got some time to kill."

"Sure! How many big spenders do I know? Why did Romolo want to put Joe away?"

I shrugged. "Let's go to Al's Alley. We can bowl a couple of games and drink a couple Einlichers and then I'll buy you a steak at Heinie's."

"You're not going home?" He smiled. "You don't think the Feds guessed right?"

"I never second-guess God. Let's go."

We rolled three games and drank some Einlicher and had a nice, greasy pan-fried steak at Heinie's. I wished him luck and went over to Ocean Avenue early. If her place was staked out, if the law was waiting for me, I'd go home without seeing the doctor.

There was no stakeout that I noticed. When the

DeVille turned into the alley a few minutes before six-thirty, I waited to see if any car had been following it.

None had. I left my car parked on the entry street and walked up the alley and up the outside steps to her second-floor apartment.

The door to her apartment opened directly into the living room. Mary Bettis said, "Come in."

I came in. For the second time that day, nobody asked me to sit down. "This is Dr. Darius," she said.

He was of medium height, but wide. He had a broad olive-skinned face and short black hair studded with gray. He could have been forty or sixty.

"I checked you out," he said.

"That was wise. You should have done the same with Puma."

"I couldn't. He didn't pretend to be honest. What do you want from me?"

"I came here to find out if you remodeled the face of a man named Lester Hardin."

He said nothing, staring at me.

"I don't know if it's hit the news yet," I said, "but the government men have already arrested the hoodlums who killed Puma. I'm sure they don't know you're the man who told Puma what you don't want to tell me."

"Is that a threat, Mr. Callahan?"

"Read it any way you want. I guarantee you the Feds will never learn you told me, if you cooperate."

"And if I don't cooperate?"

"Then we might never know who killed Puma. I think the government men are wrong. If they are, that could be a *real* threat to you."

He looked at Mary, and back at me. "I performed facial surgery on a man named Lester Hardin."

"Thank you. Do you have a picture of the way he looks now? Isn't that a customary practice, the before-and-after pictures?"

"Rarely, in my practice. I am not a quack, Mr. Callahan. I have no picture of him, before or after, and no knowledge of where he is now or what name he's using. And that is all you will learn from me."

"I think it's enough. Sorry for the intrusion." I nodded, and turned toward the door.

"Wait!" he said. "What's your stake in this?"

"A man has been killed," I said, "and his killer was breathing free air. For Christ's sake, do I have to explain that to a doctor?"

I left them on that noble note. He wasn't a quack, he had said. Doctors have their private insular code of ethics. In a suffering, sick world he used his fine skills to rebuild the noses of movie stars. And he wasn't a quack? They have their own lexicon.

I filled the car with gas at a self-serve station and headed for home. The government operatives would be packing up and leaving town. The Justice Department attorneys would take over.

A couple of hoodlums would spend three or four years in courts, supported by taxpayers, defended by expensive lawyers who must not be called shysters. Lawyers, too, have their own lexicon.

Screw 'em all but six and save them for pall-bearers. What was it to me? Vindictive retribution, that's what it was to me.

It started to rain again as I was leaving Ventura. One of those frustrating misty drippers that won't turn into honest rain or go away. Screw you, too, Mother Nature.

Jan must have seen my headlights. She was waiting in the open doorway when I got there. "What happened? Bernie told me you were on the way home six hours ago."

"Screw Bernie," I said.

"Oh, boy! We're in a mood again. What happened?"

"Nothing I want to talk about now. Did you nail Madame Vulgar Taste?"

"Signed, sealed and about to be delivered. Come in out of the rain. I'll make you a drink."

"Why don't you make us some cocoa? Some hot rich cocoa? Make it with cream."

"That's too rich. I'll make it with Half-and-Half. Go sit down and try to relax."

Home is the hunter, home from the hills. I sat in the den and tried to relax. With all their sophisticated equipment, their manpower, their official clout, the Feds had come up with Rodney and Arvid Patulski from Detroit. Maybe they had a case.

Al Capone had probably killed more people than Genghis Khan. They had finally nailed Al— for income tax evasion. Whether they had the wrong man or the wrong reasons, the Feds could build a case.

When Jan brought my cocoa she said, "You shouldn't be angry with Bernie. He was worried about you, Brock."

"Really? He threatened to have the Santa Monica police pick me up."

"Why?"

"It's complicated and private. He was just playing cop. That's what he is, remember, a cop."

"And your good friend."

"Yes. This is great cocoa. Nobody makes cocoa better than you do. I'm glad you're mine. Are you glad I'm yours?"

"Most of the time. 'Barney Miller' will be on in a few minutes. Should I turn on the tube?"

We were halfway through it when the phone rang. I felt as if I were in a time warp. This case had started when I had interrupted Vogel in the middle of "Barney Miller."

"How come you're not watching 'Barney Miller'?" I asked him.

"Our cable is out. What did you learn down south?"

"Let's see— Well, that seventeenth hole at Riviera is a real bitch. And the fairways were so soggy I didn't get any roll, and—"

"Cut the cheap crap!" he said. "I'm asking you an official question."

"I'll give you a taxpayer's answer. I didn't learn a damned thing the Feds didn't know—but neglected to tell us."

"What?"

"Ask them. I don't reveal government secrets. I'll tell you what I'll do. I'll clear it with them first."

"You do that. Delamater's still in town. You tell him that you learned what he knows. You can share a cell with the Patulski brothers if you tell him where you were."

"Give me his phone number. We'll see."

"Oh, God—"

I laughed. "I'm calling you, Bernie. Turn over your hole card and show me your deuce."

"You bastard," he said.

"Right. Your bastard buddy. Tomorrow we'll talk. Okay? I've had a lousy day."

"Okay. Tomorrow we'll talk. Ten o'clock in my office."

"Yes, sir."

Back in the den Jan said, "The way you two treat each other!"

"It's our macho way of hiding our affection," I explained. "What's bugging Barney?"

"He's getting a divorce. He's moved to a hotel. But Mrs. Miller keeps dropping in at the station with a lot of phony excuses. I think she realizes now what a wonderful man she has. Or had."

"Let that be a lesson to you," I said. "I'm going to soak in a hot tub."

Soaking and thinking, sorting out my priorities. It would be comforting to see Rodney and Arvid behind bars. It would be more comforting to watch them roasting over a slow fire but both

Sloan and I realized that was a hyperbolical fantasy.

If the Feds ever learned that Darius had been responsible for blowing their witness's cover, he would be in deep trouble. That was okay with me. But Mary Bettis, too? That was not okay with me.

Calvin was my vindictive retribution blood brother. That ornery little bastard had forced himself to live so that he could get even. He hadn't lied to Bernie and me. He had saved that for the Feds. Bernie should realize that. He wasn't dumb. Maybe Bernie also believed in vindictive retribution—if it was legal.

Justice or the law? You have to stay with the law. There are too many disparate views of justice. The law was black and white, in print, founded on precedent, hammered out through the experience of troubled and thoughtful men over the centuries.

But subject to interpretation, full of loopholes, judged by black-robed men with deep personal prejudices and often inadequate schooling or mental lacks. How could these men expect a citizen to respect the law when they rarely—if ever—sent rich murderers to the execution chambers? More then half of the creeps involved in Watergate had been lawyers, including the attorney general. These men were supposed to be officers of the court. Some court!

From the other side of the bathroom door, Jan asked, "Did you drown? What are you doing in there?"

"Soaking and thinking. I'll be out in a couple of minutes."

"Okay. There's a lot of cocoa left and an old Bogart movie starting pretty soon on Channel Five."

Cocoa and an old Bogart movie, far from smogtown, sitting with my own true love in our snug den out of the rain. Don't sulk, you dumb Irishman, ninety-nine percent of the people in the world would trade places with you.

**21**

THE WIND HAD SHIFTED during the night; a hot santana was blowing in from the desert. Steam vapors drifted up from the waterlogged shake roofs of the houses in the neighborhood. The residents who no longer worked for a living were hauling away the sandbags they had so laboriously piled in front of their homes.

I didn't drive the Mustang down to the station. Romolo was still in town and there were other guns for hire.

Chief Harris was coming out of Bernie's office when I got there. He nodded curtly at me and went down the hall toward his office. He hadn't needed me on this one. I had brought a killer cop to justice last time I had worked with Bernie. Harris would probably never forgive me for that.

Vogel was standing by his small window, staring out—and smoking, of course.

"No paperwork?" I asked him.

"Lay off!" he said. "You overlook a lot of opportunities to keep your mouth shut."

I sat down in the old-fashioned captain's chair next to his desk. He came over to sit in his office chair. He stubbed out his cigarette in an over-loaded ashtray and coughed.

"Damn those stinking things!" he said. "I am sure one weak-willed son of a bitch."

I didn't overlook the opportunity to keep my mouth shut.

He looked at me. "Well?"

"I've been thinking about those five defense witnesses the Patulski brothers have stashed down in El Cajon. How about them?"

"The word I get from our government friends is that they have been questioned and have suddenly suffered a memory lapse. I wasn't told much more than that, but I had a feeling the Romolo family is no longer welcome in the national brotherhood."

"Could be. Peter Scarlatti thinks Tony is crazy. I guess he meant out of tune with modern mob strategy."

"How do you know what Peter Scarlatti thinks?"

"He was in our foursome at Riviera."

He stared at me. "Are you serious?"

"No. Bernie, the way it shaped up, you went your way and the Feds went theirs and I went mine. We weren't really working together, were we?"

He didn't answer.

"How about the thirty-two?" I asked him. "Did they find that?"

He shook his head. "If they do, they'll really have a case. The bullet went through Joe's eye socket and embedded in his brain. It must have been old powder. Ballistics has an almost-perfect slug. But professionals don't use the same gun twice. Who is this Dr. Darius?''

"Between us? Just you and me, sitting here alone?''

He reached for another cigarette and put it back. He took a deep breath. He said, "Yes.''

I gave him the whole story with one omission; I didn't mention Tracy Perlman. I told one lie: Peter had given me the name of Dr. Darius.

"Well,'' he said, "that should mean the Feds guessed right. Tony is out of the brotherhood.''

"Today, maybe. Tomorrow, maybe not.''

"Yeah. With *them*. And this Lester Hardin is here in town?''

"I guess. Should we go and look for him?''

He shook his head.'' The chief told me ten minutes ago that it was strictly federal business from here in.''

"Murder is not a federal crime, so far as I know.''

"Run in and explain that to Harris. You had a lot of guts to go down and question Scarlatti.''

"I had a letter of introduction and a solid character reference from Mrs. Puma.''

"Puma was going to finger this Hardin for Tony?''

"I don't know.''

"You don't want to know. He's one of yours.''

"Get off that red-neck cop kick, will you? That's not the real you, for Christ's sake!''

Nothing from him.

"How's Calvin doing?'' I asked.

"He's alive, and as ornery as ever. But I don't think he's going to make it. He's still bleeding inside. The damned fool!"

"You like him, don't you?"

"Aagh!" he said.

"Do the Feds have a guard on him?"

"We have. That's our job."

"I wonder if I could talk with him?"

"Why?"

"Because I like him, too. Could you maybe arrange it?"

"Ask the chief."

"Bernie!"

"Okay. The man at the door right now is the one you talked with in front of Puma's house. I guess he knows you."

"Not the lard ass?"

"No. The other one. I'll phone the hospital."

Loreli General was only five or six blocks from the station. I walked. The Feds had their case and Bernie was no longer involved in it. Why was I?

The uniformed man at the door had a big smile for me. "Did you solve this one for Bernie, too?"

"Most of it. Calvin holding up?"

"That little bastard? He's too mean to die."

They were giving Calvin both plasma and glucose through needles in his arms.

"Buddy," he said. "Did you bring me a snort?"

He looked awful, his face discolored, his lips puffed and distorted.

"You con man," I said. "You lied to the Feds, didn't you? You were trying to blackmail Romolo."

"Talk nice. I'm sick, man!"

"And you lied about Puma. You didn't see it happen."

His puffed lips twisted in a grotesque attempt at a smile. "My daddy told me something once I never forgot. He told me it would be a wonderful world if milk would stay sweet as long as revenge."

"They have memories, Calvin. The Feds can't hide you from them forever. They'll get to you."

"They'd better hurry. I ain't got long."

"Stop it! The doctors think you're improving."

"What do they know? They're almost as dumb as cops."

"You're not going to level with me, are you?"

He shook his head.

"You get better," I said. "When you're strong enough, I'll sneak a couple snorts in for you. Dwell on that. Anything you want now?"

He shook his head. "What I want, I'm going to get. Revenge. If I was stronger, we could play a little gin."

"Get stronger. Work on it!"

"Sure. Don't do nothing foolish, buddy. Don't keep nosing around. We got the guys we want."

"Even though they're innocent?"

"Innocent? Of what? Shit, man, they ain't been innocent since they left the cradle. Overdue, that's what they are. Don't you believe in justice?"

In an uncertain world it must be a relief to be as certain about anything as cantankerous Calvin Ellers was. He had too often been a victim of what the law called justice; he had been forced to find his own definition. He had followed the Kennedy dictum; never get mad, get even. On this one, Calvin had decided he would be judge, jury and executioner.

His moral case was sound enough; they *were* overdue. They had killed and gone free. Capone had been slapped on the wrist with an income tax violation. Al was lucky Calvin hadn't been the judge on his case.

So what's your problem, Callahan? Have you deserted your code of vindictive retribution? Come on, I told the inner me, that was arrogant nonsense and you know it.

Calvin had gone through his soliloquy and decided the Patulski brothers were not to be.

I went back to the station and Bernie was still there. "Any deals being offered by the defense?" I asked him.

"Tentative. They'll plead guilty to aggravated assault on Calvin. But murder? Nope."

"What would aggravated assault get them?"

"With their records? Maybe fifteen years—with fourteen and a half years off for good behavior. What did Calvin have to say?"

"Not much. The same old con. I guess he's ready for the fires of hell if Rodney and Arvid make the trip with him."

"Crazy man! He finally got in over his head."

"So did they. Come on, I'll take you to lunch and cheer you up."

He shook his head. "I'm eating at home. I'm starting my vacation today. I came in this morning only to clean up some paperwork."

I phoned Kay Decor from his office to see if I could buy Jan a lunch, but she was back in the Santa Ynez Valley, probably nailing old Vulgar Taste to the cross.

I went home. Mrs. Casey was washing clothes. "I didn't expect you home for lunch," she explained.

"Don't worry about it. I can make my own."

"No, you can't. No man is going to mess up *my* kitchen. I'll fix up something in a jiffy."

Sloan and I, bossed by irreplaceable women. I took a cold bottle of Einlicher out to the patio with me. Lies and red herrings, blind trails and false leads, while the obvious had jeered at me.

At the county jail I had asked Joe what he was doing these days. Whatever makes a buck, he had told me. He had extended his whatever too far. He should have stayed with bail bonds.

Motive, means and opportunity, that's what the prosecutor must show to prove guilt in a murder trial. The Feds didn't have the gun, which was the means. Calvin had convinced them the Patulski's had the opportunity. The motive? If they went into court and established the motive, Lester Hardin's cover would be on the public record.

Nobody was paying me and it was none of my business. After lunch I gathered up the Puma papers and put them into an old cardboard-box file of mine. This case was closed.

Vogel was going on vacation, the federal investigators were leaving town. We had the guys we wanted. I kept telling myself that. I put on my running clothes and went out for a five miler.

The first half was uphill to Vantage Rock. I was bushed by the time I got there. I hadn't done any running for a month. I stopped up there and sat on a bench and looked down on the city below.

Ocean-laved, mountain-girded San Valdesto, snug little, smug little town that had resisted growth. No new homes could be built; they would not be granted water connections. The prices of the present homes had tripled in two years. Only the rich could move here now, people as rich as Tony Romolo.

Had Tony moved here because the man who had helped jail his father lived here? Or had that been another coincidence? There had been enough of those.

The trip home was easier, downhill all the way. Twelve minutes of stretching and bending exercises after that, and I should have felt better. I only felt more tired.

Jan, too, was tired when she came home. "The ideas that woman has! I tried to listen politely, but my stomach kept churning."

"It's her money," I pointed out. "Hasn't she a right to bad taste if she's paying for it?"

"She has. But I also have a professional duty to my trade. Taste is what we sell. If she wants an ugly house, she doesn't need us. She already has that. I didn't get back into this business for the money in it."

"Okay, okay," I said soothingly. "Don't get steamed. You're right. Take off your shoes and relax. I'll make you a nice cold martini."

I have a professional duty to my trade.... I

dwelt on those words as I poured the refrigerated Beefeater into a chilled glass and tinged it with extra-dry vermouth from a converted perfume atomizer.

I poured myself three ounces of distilled corn, added ice, and took it with me to the chair flanking hers.

"How was your day?" she asked.

"Mostly physical. I ran five miles this afternoon."

"And this morning?"

"I talked with Vogel and that man the hoodlums put into the hospital."

"How is he doing?"

"He's still breathing. Only God knows for how long. The medics were sure he wouldn't last this long. Now they think he is on the road to recovery. They could be wrong twice on the same case."

"And I," Jan said, "come home complaining about a woman with bad taste. You must think I am the world's most trivial nitwit."

"Nope. I adore you. And I admire your professionalism."

She looked at me suspiciously.

"Scout's honor," I said. "You have helped me decide what I must do tonight."

"What's that?"

"I must see a man."

## 22

I HAD PHONED HIM FROM HOME; Stu Engelke
opened the front door before I had a chance to
ring. "Come in," he said. "Something new on the
murder?" His voice was tight.

"I don't know. That's why I'm here."

He led me into the small room where Nadia and
I had shared the Wild Turkey. She was sitting on
the same hassock. She nodded as I came in, nothing more.

I sat in the same leather chair. Stu asked,
"Drink?"

I shook my head. "Are you Lester Hardin?" I
asked him.

"Did Delamater tell you that?"

"No."

"Who, then?"

"A number of things. Some lies, some inform-
ants. Why did you tell me Livorno Investments
owned a big block of stock in South Coast? They
owned five hundred shares, which they sold yesterday."

He didn't answer.

I looked at Nadia. "And you told me one of
Stu's attorney friends told you Puma kept trail-

ing Stu after those first two days. How would a corporation attorney know that? You were worried about it weren't you? But if you mentioned the Feds had told you, you'd be revealing too much to me."

She, too, didn't answer.

Stu looked at her and back at me. "What's your point, Brock? If you know I'm Lester Hardin, you must know now why we lied. What's your involvement now? The killers have been found and they're going to be tried."

"Maybe they're not the real killers."

He frowned. "What are you saying? You think that Ellers lied about that?"

"I know he did. He as much as admitted it to me this morning."

"Why would he lie to the police?"

"For revenge on those men who put him into intensive care."

"And you didn't tell Vogel that, or Delamater?"

I shook my head.

"In that case," he said, "I think we had better tell Delamater right now. He's still in town. I'll phone him."

"Hear me out, first."

"Why? Delamater should be here. This is federal business. They have a right to know."

"Hear him out," Nadia said.

He stared at her and looked doubtfully back at me. "Go on."

"Puma was killed with a thirty-two," I said, "an unusual gun for a professional to be carrying. Evidently the cartridges were old, the powder deteriorated. That would *never* happen with a professional." I paused. This was the nasty part. I asked, "Do you have a thirty-two?"

His face showed neither guilt nor fear, only shock. "What kind of question is that?"

"Do you?"

"I do. Delamater suggested I buy a gun eight years ago, in case I might need it. I've never used it. Did you come here tonight to accuse me of murder?"

"In self-defense, to save your life, why not?"

He said coldly, "The night Puma was shot I was in San Diego at a convention of California utility companies."

I stood up. "Okay. I guessed wrong. I had to ask. I don't even know why. It's none of my damned business, but I had to ask."

His voice was dead flat. "You can check that San Diego convention story easily enough. And I suppose the police still have the slug that killed Puma?"

I nodded. "Ballistics has it."

"I'll give you the gun," he said. "They can check it. That much, I guess, I owe you." He went toward the door.

"No," Nadia said.

He turned and stared at her. She was huddled on the hassock, her head down. She didn't look up to meet his stare.

"You?" he asked.

She nodded.

"My God! What—why?"

She looked up. "He found out who you were."

"How?"

"I don't know. I went to his office that afternoon. I wanted to make sure he hadn't kept a record of that silly—" She took a deep breath. "He was talking on the phone in his inner office. It's only a five-foot partition. I could hear what he was saying. He told the other person the man he wanted was due back from San Diego tomorrow. He wanted his money tonight, thirty thousand dollars. The other man's house was being watched, I guess, so Mr. Puma suggested they meet behind that filling station on Arroyo Road."

"Why didn't you phone Delamater?"

"Why? Has he protected us so well?" She looked at me. "We've moved three times in the last eight years." She took another deep breath. "I went home. I decided I would offer him sixty thousand dollars. I phoned him at his office. He wasn't there. I kept phoning his office and his home and never got an answer." She broke off, and started to cry.

"Jesus!" Stu said.

"Tell us the rest, Nadia," I said gently.

She was huddled again, her eyes closed. "I got there before those men did. I told him I'd double their offer, I'd triple it. He tried to tell me at first it had nothing to do with Stu. Then he said it was his life or Stu's; he couldn't double-cross hoodlums. And I had better get out of there; they were due to meet him in a few minutes."

Stu said, "But you took the gun along. You had plenty of time to warn me, Nadia."

She looked up. Her eyes were fierce, her voice harsh. "So we could start running again?"

Stu looked at me, back at his wife, and again at me.

I said, "Why don't we all have a nice double shot of Wild Turkey and forget I was ever here?"

"Are you crazy?" Stu said. "Those men are innocent!"

"That's what I told Calvin Ellers in the hospital. His answer was that they weren't. What they were was overdue. I've decided Calvin's answer is my answer."

Stu shook his head. "No, no—"

"Grow up, Stu. Delamater knows you own a thirty-two. Did he ask you about it? Did he ever ask you where you were that night?"

"Why should he?"

"Why shouldn't he? I did. This isn't murder, man. It's justifiable homicide. Are you going to pour, or am I going home dry?"

He came around before I left. How long a lawyer could keep that kind of secret from the law was something I couldn't judge. As a nonlawyer, married to Nadia, I could have carried it to my grave.

They would move again, probably. I suggested Pasa Robles, close enough so we could visit, secluded enough so that Romolo might take longer to find them. If Tony was outside the brotherhood now, maybe he'd be hiding, too.

It was only nine-thirty; the Pumas should still be up. Under a full moon, I drove through the exclusive area and across the overpass to the less-exclusive area of tract homes.

Joey opened the door. "Have you heard the news? It just came over the radio."

"What news?"

"That witness died. Calvin Ellers."

Good night, sour prince.... "I didn't hear it," I said, "but I expected it."

"Mom's in the kitchen. Want some coffee?"

"A sound idea. I came here to tell you the story you may never read. There'll be a million rumors. I want you to get it straight."

In the kitchen, at the breakfast-nook end, Ellen Puma was busily typing on a portable machine. The table was covered with papers.

"Is the boss paying you overtime for home typing?" I asked her.

She smiled. "He can't afford it. Not yet. But I'm going to make him rich. He is one bright star." She began to pick up the papers and put them into a manila folder. "Sit down. There's coffee on."

When we were all settled with our coffee, she asked, "With that witness dead will the F.B.I. still have a case?"

"Stronger than ever. Ellers identified both men. And they had already admitted they beat him up."

"They were working for Romolo, weren't they?"

I nodded.

"And that's why they killed Joe, because of their feud with the Scarlattis?"

I shook my head. "Not completely. Though the animosity between those families probably culminated in what...happened to him. Somehow Joe found out enough to make him suspect that the man who testified against Nick Romolo was living in town under a new name."

Joey stared at me. "And dad was going to finger him for Tony Romolo?"

"No way! Did Romolo ever send your dad a Christmas check?"

Joey continued to stare at me, doubt on his face. He looked at his mother, took a deep breath and looked again at me. "Then what about the thirty thousand dollars?"

"What thirty thousand dollars?" Ellen asked. "What are you talking about, Joey?"

"One of Joe's pipe dreams probably," I answered for him. "We all have them in the trade. The only way I can figure it, he must have thought there was a reason Tony Romolo came to town and the reason could be he was going to waste the witness who had put his father in the can."

"And?"

"And he could have figured that kind of information could be useful to Peter. The mob is more subtle now. One thing they don't need is vindictive gang violence. They've gone legitimate. If Peter could convince the brotherhood that Tony was an anachronism...."

Ellen nodded.

"But first," I went on, "Joe had to make sure this man in town was what he suspected. He went down to Los Angeles and made sure by questioning the surgeon who had made the man a new face."

"And he took that information to Peter?"

"He did. But Peter told me he didn't ask for a nickel. I guess Joe figured Peter had done enough for him. There was still the problem of law school. That's when he took out the insurance."

"You mean he *knew* he was going to die?"

"No. But there was the risk. And the odds were right for a horse player. Term insurance is the best bet for the money."

"That fool," Ellen said hoarsely. "That crazy man!"

"That crazy *gutty* man," I said.

"But mostly crazy," she said. "Meeting hoodlums in a place as deserted as that?"

"He didn't meet them there. They had some woman phone him on the pretext she was a prospective client. Romolo's men picked him up in the parking lot of the restaurant where he was supposed to meet the woman and took him to that lot where he might not be found for a while."

Silence. Joey took his mother's hand in his. Silence.

"None of this will be in the papers, of course," I explained. "It would blow the witness's cover."

"But how," Ellen asked, "did Romolo learn that Joe had uncovered the witness?"

I shrugged. "They have sources of information not available to citizens. They might have been tipped off by that cosmetic surgeon. We'll never know."

"And the stooges will be tried," Joey said, "and Tony Romolo won't be touched. I think I'll buy a gun."

"They have the guns, Joey. You go to law school and get your own gun. As for Tony Romolo, the word I get is that he's likely to suffer Mafia justice. It's quicker and cheaper. Peter is still a power and Peter thought an awful lot of Joe."

"God!" Ellen said. "What a world we live in!"

"It's not our world," I said. "Is that a fresh apple pie on the counter?"

"Still warm from the oven," she said. "Would you like a piece?"

"Sure would. Maybe with a scoop of vanilla ice cream on top? That's our world, Ellen."

"Eek!" she said. "You must watch 'The Waltons.' "

I nodded sadly and humbly. "I'm like Tony, an anachronism."

"Like hell," she said. "You know what you are? You are an avenging angel."

We had that with another cup of coffee and they thanked me and I assured them it was nothing, glad to be of help, forget it, and I went out into the bright moonlit night.

Liar, liar, your pants are on fire. . . . This time I didn't even feel guilty about not feeling guilty. I had to survive, didn't I? How could I bring order to a disorderly world if I didn't survive?

Little white lies in a black world—but all in the cause of justice, all on the side of the angels.

I would do my penance on the picket line, carrying one of those dumb signs in a lost cause. Lost causes were my specialty. Thank God for Uncle Homer. Thank God he had died rich.

You win some, you lose some, as Lenny had said. But nobody wins the big one.

Always remember that.

*Be a detective.*
*See if you can solve . . .*

# Raven House
## MINUTE
## MYSTERY #4

On the following page is Raven House
MINUTE MYSTERY #4, "A Sound Sleeper."

**Every** month each Raven House book will feature a
MINUTE MYSTERY, a unique little puzzler designed
to let *you* do the sleuthing!

U.S. (except Arizona) residents may check the answer
by calling **1-800-528-1404** anytime from March 1 to
May 15, 1982. U.S. residents may also obtain the solution
by writing anytime during or after this period to:

Raven House MINUTE MYSTERY
1440 South Priest Drive
Tempe, AZ 85281

Canadian residents, please write to the following
address:

Raven House MINUTE MYSTERY
649 Ontario Street
Stratford, Ontario N5A 6W2

From Minute Mysteries by Austin Ripley.
Copyright © 1948 by Opera Mundi, Paris.

# A SOUND SLEEPER

Professor Fordney's attention was attracted by a suspicious-looking bulge in the right pocket of an obviously expensive camel's-hair overcoat, which was thrown carelessly over Skamp's green coat.

"That yours?" he asked John London.

"Yes, sir. You see. . . ."

"Just a moment," interrupted the professor. A rather sheepish grin spread over his face when he found the bulge in the coat was made by a large peppermint candy cane. Examining the green coat, a sudden thought struck him. Perhaps that cane did have some significance!

He had already seen the body of Henry Skamp lying on the floor of the one-room apartment. Skamp had been stabbed.

"All right," Fordney nodded to London, "continue."

"Last night Henry came home a bit drunk, woke me up, and when I refused to listen to him tell about his love affair, he flung his coat on that chair and lay down beside me fully dressed. I was tired and went right back to sleep. When I awoke this morning— around nine o'clock—I found hi... lying there dead and called the police."

"You heard no sound after you went to sleep the second time, and you disturbed nothing?" the professor inquired.

"No—I was dead tired."

"How long have you two been roommates?"

"Oh, quite a while. About two years. I forgot to tell you that three months ago Henry lost his job and he's been brooding ever since."

"H'mm. . . ." Fordney pondered a moment. "You're lying, London. I'm holding you on suspicion!"

*How did the professor know London was lying?*

From **Minute Mysteries** by Austin Ripley.
Copyright © 1949 by Opera Mundi, Paris.